He thought he saw ~~~~~~~ ~~~~~~~~
as if it were brea~~~~~~~~~~~~~, he decided that
his eyes were playing tricks on him. He looked
again, and what he'd thought was part of the tree
was really a smooth, naked, dark back . . . and
long dark hair . . . and the side of a wonderfully
rounded buttock.

He froze as the girl turned toward him. She was
unfamiliar to him: not from town, not from the
housing development. Her eyes were blank, her
mouth expressionless, her naked beauty exquisite.

"Yes, sir," she said mechanically. "Yes, sir."
She repeated his earlier words in a voice that
sounded exactly like his. It was a perfect imitation
that could come only from the devil himself.

As he slowly raised his rifle to a firing position,
the girl vanished. He screamed then – a high-
pitched animal-like scream that was immediately
repeated around him . . .

Also by T. M. Wright in Gollancz Horror

THE ISLAND

A MANHATTAN GHOST STORY

THE WAITING ROOM

THE PLACE

THE LAST VAMPIRE

THE SCHOOL

BOUNDARIES

LITTLE BOY LOST

STRANGE SEED

T.M. WRIGHT

NURSERY TALE

GOLLANCZ HORROR

First VG Horror edition published 1994
by Victor Gollancz
A Cassell imprint
Villiers House, 41/47 Strand, London WC2N 5JE

© T. M. Wright 1982

A catalogue record for this book is
available from the British Library.

ISBN 0 575 05508 1

Printed and bound in Great Britain
by Cox & Wyman Ltd, Reading, Berks

In memory of John Lennon

Acknowledgments

Thanks to Bill Thompson, who helped bring *Strange Seed* into the world. And to Stephen King, one of the few who understood it. And Mike Cantalupo, who has always had a kind word, and sound advice. And Sharon Jarvis, without whom . . . Later thanks also to Jack Garner, for being candid.

Be fruitful, and multiply, and replenish the earth and subdue it: and have dominion over the fish of the sea, and over the fowl of the air, and over every living thing that moveth upon the earth.

—GENESIS I:28

Part One

GROUNDWORK

From *The Penn Yann Post Gazette,* December 6:

COUPLE INCINERATED IN HOUSE FIRE

Paul Griffin, 30, and his wife Rachel, 26, were killed last night in a fire at their 100-year-old farmhouse on the Tripp Road extension, ten miles north of Penn Yann. According to Deputy Volunteer Fire Chief Clyde Watkins, the fire apparently started when a gasoline-powered electric generator at the side of the house exploded. Watkins described the destruction caused by the fire as "total," and added that when he and his men arrived on the scene at approximately 3:15 A.M., the Griffin house was completely engulfed in flames.

According to Penn Yann resident John Marsh—who did occasional work for the Griffins—the couple had moved into the farmhouse about six months ago, hoping to make the farm profitable once again. "But there were lots of problems," Marsh explained. "I remember when they first moved in, for instance; that house was a shambles. Vandals got in there and just went wild."

Investigation has revealed that the house's previous owners, a middle-aged couple named Schmidt, were found dead at the house in August, 1972, apparently as the result of a double suicide. Prior to that tragedy, Paul Griffin's father, Samuel Griffin, one-time owner of the house, died of a heart attack there in 1957.

Mr. Griffin, formerly of New York City, leaves an uncle, Harold Martinson. His wife leaves her mother and father, two sisters, several aunts and uncles, nieces and nephews. No local service is planned.

From *The Penn Yann Post Gazette*, April 3:

COMPLAINT FILED IN CASE OF MISSING MAN

Mrs. Maureen Collins, of Syracuse, New York, has filed a complaint charging that local Police Chief John Hastings and his men were "negligent and incompetent" in their investigation of the disappearance of Mrs. Collins's husband, Mark, in January of this year. Mark Collins apparently disappeared while on a hunting expedition with several friends in the Tripp Road area, about ten miles from Penn Yann.

Says Mrs. Collins, "Those people"—Police Chief Hastings and his men—"didn't spend more than two days looking for my husband. And they didn't call in anyone from outside. It was obvious they didn't expect to find him, or

they didn't want to." Mrs. Collins, who is
white, has also alleged racism on the part of
Police Chief Hastings in the search for her
husband, who is a black man. Chief Hastings
stated "no comment" when asked about the
complaint.

Chapter 1

August

The boy, squinting in the late afternoon country sunlight, looked up briefly at the man beside him and nodded to his left, at the remains of a cellar and some blackened timbers strewn about. "Hey, Grandpa," the boy said, "there was a house there once. Looks like it burned up."

"Burned down," the man corrected.

"Huh?"

"It burned down. It didn't burn up, it burned down."

"Oh." The boy didn't understand. "Anybody get killed, ya think?"

"You're a morbid sort, aren'tcha?"

"Morbid?" The boy's eyebrows wrinkled. "What's that mean?"

"It means you want all the gory details." The man chuckled softly. "Yeah," he continued after a moment, and there was a tiny note of solemnity in

17

his voice. "People got killed. A man and his wife—
back-to-the-landers, they were."

"What's—" the boy started, and the man, antici-
pating him, cut in, "Tryin' to find their roots in the
earth. And no, they weren't trees, if that's what
you were gonna say."

"I wasn't gonna say nothin', Grandpa."

"Uh-huh, and bears don't crap in the woods,
either."

"They don't?"

The man laughed. "Sure they do. Where else
they gonna crap if not in the woods?"

The boy understood. He grinned because his
grandpa was sharing such a great joke with him; it
was at times like these that the boy felt especially
close to the man.

"D'ja know the people who got killed in that
house, Grandpa?"

The man stopped walking; the boy stopped. "I
knew *of* 'em, son. I knew of 'em." And the boy
noticed something strange and quiet in his voice,
something that said, *Let's forget it, for now.*

The boy took the man's hand and squeezed it
affectionately. "Supper's 'bout ready, don'tcha
think?" It took a moment for the man to answer:
"Uh-huh. Probably past ready." And they started
walking again.

Several minutes later, when they had completed
half their walk, they turned and started back the
way they'd come. The sun was low on the horizon
now, and the boy sensed that his grandpa had
quickened the pace.

"Yer walkin' pretty fast, Grandpa."

"Am I?"

"Yeah. You must be awful hungry, huh?"

"Famished."

" 'Famished'? Does that mean hungry?"

"It means you talk enough for five little kids."

"I'm sorry." The boy sounded hurt; he felt the man's arm around his shoulders. "*Ten* little kids," the man said, and he chuckled falsely. The boy silently accepted the apology.

They soon passed the spot where the house had been and the boy said enthusiastically, "Hey, Grandpa, why don't we just cut through there." He pointed at a narrow weathered path that ran at right angles to the road they were on and apparently ended at a stand of deciduous trees not quite a half mile off. The setting sun made the trees appear to be on fire; the boy liked that. "We could be back home and sittin' down to supper in a couple minutes, I bet," he continued, and grinned, pleased that he could save his grandpa some walking time. He felt the man's grip tighten around his shoulders.

"Shouldn'ta brought you here, son," he said. "I don't know what I was thinkin', don't know what I was thinkin' at all, but I shouldn'ta brought you here."

The boy didn't understand. "Yer hurtin' me. What'sa matter, Grandpa?"

The man loosened his grip, then quickened his pace even more, so that the boy had to do a half walk, half run to keep up. "Grandpa, you scared a somethin'? What you scared of?"

The man said nothing. But now he *was* running, and the boy found terror growing inside himself, found that he was glancing frantically about for a *reason* to run, found that—worst of all—the man was rapidly outdistancing him. "Grandpa, wait. Please!" He saw the man glance back, saw the terror and confusion on the old face. "Grandpa, stop!" But the man didn't stop.

The boy had never realized how really fast his legs could move. He remembered fleetingly, almost wistfully, as he ran, the time a year and a half earlier when he had been in the woodsy section of a city park and had convinced himself that a bear was rooting about in some nearby bushes. He had run as fast—he supposed later—as any boy, or man, or *thing* had *ever* run, and for months afterward his dreams had been filled with wonderful, fantastic memories of it.

But that was in the past, he realized now. And there had been nothing real about it.

This was real! The terror and confusion and panic on his grandpa's face, and the distance opening up between them, and the thing—whatever it was—that they were running from . . .

The boy fell very quickly, too quickly for his hands to react and cushion him. His chin hit the gravel first, and a small, sharp stone opened up an inch-long gash; then his forehead, chest and legs hit. "Grand–" he managed as he hit. Then he heard a muffled, dry, grunting sound.

Moments later, he was unconscious.

"You'll tell me the truth, Earl Freeman, or I'll know the reason why."

Earl Freeman glanced blankly at his wife, then just as blankly at the boy lying quietly on the old bed. They had sent for the doctor, but it was a ten-mile drive from town, and most of that was over bad, one-lane, unpaved roads. He turned away, walked to a window, looked out. "We were running, like I said."

"I *know* what you said, and I *know* there's more."

It was something greater than hate that Earl Freeman felt for himself, now—had felt ever since, in a panic, he had scooped the boy up from the road. More than hate. More like a certainty that his actions in the last hour had loudly denied his very worth as a human being. "We were on Griffin's Road," he said, and closed his eyes briefly, happy that he'd admitted it at last.

He heard his wife sit very slowly in a chair she'd brought in from the kitchen and had put near the bed. After a long moment, she whispered, "Why, Earl?"

But Earl Freeman couldn't answer the question—not, at least, in a rational way. The late afternoon walk had been planned for the Tripp Road, not Griffin's Road. He supposed, very briefly, that—where the two roads met, a mile from the house—he had inadvertently taken a left when he should not have turned at all. But that was no good, because he *remembered* turning, remembered knowing *where* he was taking Seth, remembered passing the remains of the house—passing, and walking to the end of Griffin's Road, where the fields started, remembered *knowing* they would have to pass the house again, when darkness was beginning . . .

"I don't know," he whispered, and from his tone his wife realized it was the very best he could do.

She said, "Why were you running, Earl?" She paused only a moment. "Did you have a reason, was there some *reason*?"

"No," he murmured. "No . . ."

"Earl," she cut in, nodding urgently at the boy in the bed. "I think he's coming around."

Earl Freeman went to the side of the bed. He

looked anxiously at Seth. The boy's eyes fluttered open. "Seth?" Earl Freeman said. The boy's eyes stayed open. "Seth, you're home now." Wide open. Unfocused, and uncomprehending.

Earl Freeman heard his wife breathe, "Oh my God!"

"Seth, you're home now!" Quickly, desperately. "You're home now!"

Seth remained quiet. His breathing was slow and deep, as if he were sleeping.

"Seth," said Earl Freeman, "what do you see? Tell me what you see."

"Earl, don't . . ." his wife began, and stopped when he put his hand on hers and whispered, "Please."

But Seth remained quiet. For the next five years.

From *The Penn Yann Post Gazette,* October 12, two years later:

TRUCK DRIVER INJURED

Luis Alvarez, 32, of Rochester, New York, suffered a broken arm, cracked pelvis, and various cuts and bruises yesterday when the truck he was driving skidded off the Tripp Road extension, popularly known as Griffin's Road, about ten miles north of Penn Yann, and flipped over, landing on its roof. According to Alvarez, who works for the Pittman Construction Company and was hauling lumber to the site of a housing development in Penn Yann at the time of the accident, he swerved off the road to avoid hitting a child who had run out in front of his truck. Alvarez explained, "One moment the road is clear, and the next moment there is this kid right in front of me, about 20 feet away. I don't know where he came from." A thorough search of the area by Penn Yann police proved fruitless. Alvarez, recovering in the Penn Yann Memorial Hospital, has been charged with carrying an unsafe load, according to Penn Yann police.

From *The Penn Yann Post Gazette*, February 22, one year later:

GO-AHEAD GIVEN FOR CONTROVERSIAL HOUSING DEVELOPMENT

After several years of often bitter controversy, and after the granting of numerous waivers to existing zoning ordinances, the Zoning Board of Penn Yann has okayed a final rezoning proposal by New York City entrepreneur Rowland Reynolds for the Tripp Road and Tripp Road extension (known as Griffin's Road), about ten miles north of Penn Yann. The rezoning will allow Reynolds to develop a 60-acre site on the extension as a "small, planned community of large, two-story residences, with at least one half-acre per residence."

The proposal, which had been delayed for five years pending a series of environmental impact statements, also requested a widening and repaving of both the extension, which is now a gravel road, and Tripp Road itself, a narrow, two-lane road which will become a major four-lane highway as construction progresses.

After the decision was handed down by the

Board, Reynolds said, "Now we can get on with the business of growth—which is what we, as a people, are all about. We have put all the rumors to rest, we have answered the extreme environmentalists, and the no-growth advocates, and those who seek more government control, and, as well, the dilettantes who would put even the things that slither about on the ground before the needs of men. And now we will do what Americans have always done best—we will make the land work for us. Because we are, after all, its caretakers. Because God has given the land to us for our use, and our enjoyment as his children."

According to Reynolds, construction will begin immediately.

Part Two

THE PEOPLE

Chapter 2

August 15, five years after the Freeman accident

Janice and Miles McIntyre

It had looked like a magnificent game of tag; now, Janice McIntyre thought she should have known better. She nudged her husband. "Miles," she said, "did you see that?" But Miles McIntyre was busy talking to the builder: "Later, darling," he said. Janice muttered, "Sorry," and moved away from him to the front of what would someday be their new home—it was now only a cellar, plywood floor, and frame ("We'll have it dried in," the builder had told them, "in a week, maybe ten days." "Dried in?" Miles had asked. "Protected from the weather." "Oh.").

Janice watched as the hawk moved gracefully through the frigid blue sky toward the stand of trees at the horizon. The thing the hawk carried in its talons was no longer recognizable. Janice had supposed, when the two birds were close to the house—"playing tag"—that it was a sparrow, but, she admitted, it could just as easily have been any other small bird. Build a house in the country, she thought, and turn into a naturalist. She felt her husband's hands on her shoulders: "There's a snag, Jan."

"A snag?"

"Yes, and it'll make you cringe, I think."

She turned around, faced him. "Okay, so make me cringe."

"They found something—"

"They?"

"The builder. Well, actually the plumbing sub-contractor—*he* found something, his men did, and they called the builder and the builder says he'll have to call the police. They were digging the hole for the septic tank"—he nodded to the north at a mound of dark, moist earth about fifty feet from the house—"over there."

"Yes?"

"And they found . . . they think they found some bones."

"Bones?"

"Human bones."

"*Human* bones?"

He hesitated, glanced away briefly, then looked back, obviously uncomfortable. "The bones of a child," he said. "That's what they think, anyway."

"Oh Jesus!"

"These people aren't, you know, qualified, I mean technically, to make a judgment like that, but—"

"I don't think I can handle this, Miles. I really don't think I can handle this!" She lowered her head and closed her eyes; he saw tears start and, despite himself, it angered him.

"Janice, it's been *five* years, and that's a *long* time—"

"Not nearly long enough, Miles. Twenty years, thirty—"

"Christ Almighty!"

"Please, Miles . . ." She quieted, closed her eyes, tried in vain to stop the tears.

Jodie—their first child—had died very suddenly, in his fifteenth month, of crib death. Jodie's doctor had apologized again and again for not having seen the child's susceptibility to Sudden Infant Death Syndrome right from the start. "We know so much more about it, now, than we did ten years ago," he told them, "but we obviously don't know nearly as much as we *need* to know." The apology had seemed, Janice thought at the time, a kind of explanation for Jodie's death, a reason for it, and it had made her very angry.

She felt the anger welling up inside her again, here, in the skeleton of what would soon be her new home. And Miles's home. And the home of the child growing inside her (it was a fact she hadn't yet shared with her husband, because she wasn't at all sure how *she* felt about it). She fought the anger down; it began to smoulder. She thought that if she spoke she would say something foolish and self-pitying, so she stayed quiet.

She stared blankly at a slowly moving speck on the horizon—the hawk and its small burden. "Damn you," she whispered. She wasn't certain what she was damning, exactly: The hawk. Miles. Maybe even Jodie.

"You want to go somewhere?" Miles asked. "To a restaurant or something? Away from here?"

She nodded yes.

Norm and Marge Gellis

Norm Gellis brought his big Mercury to a quick, jolting stop; he pointed to his right at a field of corn, each of the hundred or so rows tall and straight and ready for the harvest. Norm Gellis puffed up a little, like a bullfrog; he puffed up when he was on the verge of sharing some bit of knowledge that, it was assumed, only he was privy to. "I got it straight from Reynolds himself," he said.

His wife, a short, frail woman who often looked as if she were coming down with some awful disease, smiled tentatively. "Yes," she said. "Yes." Her voice was the only substantial thing about her—it was a ludicrous, low tenor, and it was loud, despite her attempts to control it. "Yes," she said a third time.

"And he told me," Norm Gellis continued, "he told *me* that this area here—it's about twenty-five acres, you know—is eventually going to be part of Granada. What is that? Is that corn?"

"Uh-huh," his wife answered, and immediately put on her bemused, apologetic look. *Oh, forgive me, did I say that?* the look said.

"Yeah, okay. Well, Reynolds says a lot of the farmers around here are in a real hurry to sell, if the damned government'll let 'em. Reynolds says in ten years he'll have a couple square miles and it'll all be Granada. He's got big plans, Marge. He's a doer, and we'd be missing out on a good thing if we turned him down." He paused and wondered fleetingly if Marge would misread his last remark, if she would think he was asking her permission to do what was, after all, his right and duty, as her husband, to do. "But, of course," he hurried on, "I'm not going to turn him down." He paused, reflected. "In fact," he lied, "I phoned him this morning."

Marge looked surprised. She started to speak, could think of nothing to say, and stayed quiet.

"In fact, Marge, I'm going to give him *twice* what he says he needs." He put his foot on the accelerator; the car hesitated a moment—"Damned no-lead gasoline!"—then shot forward down the narrow gravel road.

"Can we afford that?" Marge asked, her eyes on her hands clasped in her lap.

Her husband ignored the question. "Reynolds needs people like us, Marge—like you and me." He paused, thought, then went on, "You know who we are, Marge? You want to know who we are?" He was going to make a speech, Marge realized (she remembered what he had told her a dozen times: "I shoulda been a politician, Marge, because things need changin' real bad. The blacks are riotin', and the spicks are riotin', and good people are outa work, and welfare cheats are drivin' around in their Cadillacs—it's true, Marge; I seen it—and you know why all this is happenin'? I'll tell you why: Because there ain't no *discipline*. What's gotta be done is some heads have gotta be knocked around, *then* you'll see people fallin' into line.").

"Who are we, Norm?" Marge asked.

He glanced quickly, suspiciously at her. Had there been sarcasm in her question? he wondered.

"Marge," he said, "we are *the people!*" He grinned a huge, bloated grin.

Marge stayed quiet.

"And let me tell you what that means, Marge. Let me tell you what it means. It means we got *power,* I mean *real* power."

Marge listened intently for the next fifteen minutes. Every once in a while her arms and legs would tighten as her husband—caught up in the intensity of what he was saying—let the car wander dangerously close to the soft shoulder, or brought it well up past the speed limit. At the end of his speech, he sighed and grinned at her again, and she reached over and touched him affectionately. "You should have been a politician, Norm," she told him, and she thought, *It's true. He's a smart man. My husband's a very smart man—in his way!*

Dick and Trudy Wentis and their adopted son Sam

Sam Wentis closed his eyes and remembered. Had he really seen a deer five minutes ago? A real deer? It was great that they let them run loose. Maybe they let other things run loose, too—like raccoons and foxes and cows. There could even be a wild pig, or maybe a wolf in the woods behind him. Or some mountain lions. Wouldn't that be something?

He straightened a little from his crouching position in the tall quack grass. He parted the grass with his hands and squinted—because of the background of bright sky—at the two people talking and smiling fifty feet away. He could hear the drone of their voices, and found that if he cocked his head to one side, toward them, he could make out what they were saying. His hearing had always been incredibly acute.

"Just one more month," Dick Wentis said.

Trudy Wentis nodded at what, after that month, would be her very spacious backyard. "I wouldn't mind pitching a tent out here today, just so we could get away from that damned apartment."

Her husband grinned. "At one time that apartment was our dream come true, don't you remember?"

She nodded reluctantly. "Things change, Dick." She glanced about. "I think our little wild man has run off."

Dick looked about, feigning puzzlement. "You think so?" He saw the place where the grass was parted slightly, saw the splash of dark hair, and the darker eyes. He looked away and gestured slightly to his left. He said, under his breath, "We're being watched, Trudy. No, don't look."

She grinned. "I think I know one little person who very much approves of this move, Dick."

"It's no more than he deserves, Trudy. I'm glad we can give this to him. I wish . . ." He paused; she sensed his mood change. "Never mind," he continued. "Let's collect him and head home." He looked back at the place in the weeds. "Sam?" he called. "Do you think it's time to go?" The parted grass came together again; the face vanished. "Sam, do you think it's time to go?"

"I'll get him," Trudy offered.

"Okay." He pointed. "He's right over there." He called again, "Sam, c'mon, now. It'll be dark soon." He noted the hint of urgency in his tone and wondered if it bordered on impatience. He hoped not. It had been months since he'd last lost his temper with the boy. "Sam, do you think it's time to head home?"

"He's not here," Trudy called. She was standing near the spot where Dick had seen the face in the weeds. "I thought you said he was here, Dick." Her voice was trembling. "Didn't you say he was here?"

Dick started toward her. "He was right where you're standing, for God's sake!" He quickened his gait; she saw the muscles on his face tighten. "If this is another one of his goddamned tricks—"

"Dick, please—"

He stopped beside her, looked down at the trampled grass, then to his right, his left. "Sam, do you think you'd like to go home now? Do you think that would be a good idea?" He waited a moment, got no response. "Sam, we'd like to go home. What do *you* want to do?"

"Go home," he heard. His head snapped to the right.

Trudy said, confused, "That wasn't him."

Dick's gaze settled on a clump of chokecherry bushes seventy-five feet to the south. He saw movement in the bushes. "Of course it was. He's over there."

Trudy looked. "I don't see him, Dick."

"Right there, for Christ's sake!"

And Sam Wentis appeared from the chokecherry bushes. He was smiling; he looked very happy. "Yes," he said, "I think this will be fun." He stepped out of the bushes; he was tall for a ten-year-old. Trudy supposed that, fully grown, he'd be well over six feet. And he was darkly, almost hypnotically good-looking.

He moved toward his adoptive parents at a lop-ing but oddly graceful quick walk, as if he had some important business to attend to, but not so important that he would let it get in the way of his private thoughts. Trudy found it difficult to be near him without feeling great sympathy for him—he seemed to carry a special kind of deep and aching fear around with him, and at times it demanded much more of his parents than they felt they could give.

When he was several yards from them, he turned abruptly to his right and started for the car. "Aren't you coming?" he said.

"Yes," said Dick Wentis.

"Of course," said Trudy Wentis, almost at the same time, and they both fell into stride beside him.

Larry and Dora Meade and their son Timmy

John Marsh had always put sentimentality on the same shelf as grief, religion, and even love, he supposed; it was all to be taken down only when it was absolutely necessary, and until then kept tightly locked up, because *living itself* was primarily a matter of keeping somewhere in the middle of all the highs and lows. And so, when the pang of sentimentality hit him (not, he thought, unlike the feeling he might experience after eating bad meat), he tried to push it away, because it was not just distasteful, it was also a stupid waste of his valu-able time. But, at last, he had to admit, as he had admitted ten thousand times (and later denied), he was a slave to his emotions; they were far stronger than his intellect and, much of the time—now, for instance—they ran around inside him almost completely unchecked. And the big, hard bull of a man—the facade that people saw—fooled no one for very long.

He stopped his rattletrap Ford pickup on the soft shoulder of the road. He let the sentimentality sweep over him.

This was the first time in a decade and a half, ever since the fire, that he had come here. There had never been a reason, until recently; only the memories—most of them prickly and uncomfortable—and the spook stories told by nervous nellies and old men and sniggering little kids—stories that city folk might find entertaining, he supposed, but which had always been, in his estimation, just this side of outright lies. So, they had never been able to draw him back.

He hated what he saw now, on the land where the Griffins had lived and died. Hated the mounds of moist earth, the bulldozers, the yellow skeletons of houses. If only their proud new owners could look backward and see what they were replacing, what could never *be* replaced.

And then he thought, wouldn't it be something if all the spook stories were true? If Rachel and Paul Griffin—those beautiful, foolish people—still walked their land. If they still searched for whatever it was they had been searching for.

He found, suddenly, that anger was forcing itself into his sentimentality. Anger because there were no ghosts, because—said his rational view of the universe—there couldn't be. Anger that these new people and their big houses and bigger dreams trampled all over the dreams that Rachel and Paul had. Anger that there was nothing at all that he,

John Marsh, could do but stand by and watch those dreams being covered over by sparkling green lawns and clay tennis courts and circular drive-ways. Then he thought that dreams were dying everywhere, all over the world. Who was he to be angered because the Griffins' dreams had died and someone else's dreams were coming true? He had no answer for that. But he was still angry.

"You work here?" the boy said. "You a plumber or somethin'?"

Marsh turned his head quickly to the left. He saw the boy—about ten years old, blond, gray-eyed, and dressed in bright new jeans, a red flannel shirt, and bright denim jacket (the little-adult look)—standing a couple yards from the truck. The boy had taken him by surprise. Marsh smiled ingratiatingly. "Why would you wanta know? You some kinda security guard?"

"Security guard?"

"Yeah. Somebody put you in charge of looking out for strangers?"

"Huh?" The boy was puzzled.

"Because," John Marsh went on, "you never know what a stranger's going to do. He might come in here and rob everyone. Didja ever think of that?"

The boy smiled. "Is that what you're going to do? You're gonna rob us?"

John Marsh laughed deeply, infectiously (it was a laugh that had gotten him the part of Santa Claus at the Penn Yann Elementary School every Christmas for the last five years—a role that, despite his W.C. Fields image of himself, he loved). "Well, I don't know," he answered. "You got anything to rob? You got a gold watch, or a pocketful of money?"

"No," the boy answered, his voice quivering a little.

"Then I guess I can't rob *you*, can I?"

"No," the boy said again. And then, from somewhere behind him, a sharp, high-pitched female voice called, "Timmy? Where are you, Timmy?"

The boy turned a little, toward the voice, but stayed quiet.

"That your Mom?" John Marsh asked.

The boy nodded. "Uh-huh."

"Don'tcha think you should answer her?"

The boy nodded again. "Uh-huh, I guess."

"Timmy?" The voice was closer; Marsh's view of its owner was hidden by tall weeds lining the roadside. "You answer me, young man. Right now!"

"Go ahead," Marsh coaxed. "Otherwise, she'll whup ya."

Once more the boy looked puzzled. "Naw, she won't do that."

"Timmy Meade," the woman shouted—only yards away now—"you answer me this instant!"

And Marsh called, "Over here, Mrs. Meade."

A look of quick, intense anger passed from the boy to the man. Then the boy bolted into the tall weeds and was gone.

Marsh shook his head slowly, condemningly, started mumbling to himself about respect, and discipline, and parental responsibility, when a tall, harshly good-looking brunette woman appeared at the roadside. She was dressed in very tight white levis, white cotton shirt, and a white vinyl jacket. She stared hard and suspiciously at Marsh for a long moment. "Okay," she said at last, "where'd he go?"

Marsh considered a second; then, "Where'd *who* go?"

The woman raised an eyebrow. "I repeat, *where* did he go?"

Marsh grinned. "You talkin' about a little blond boy, 'bout ten years old? Had jeans on? You talking about him?"

"You know perfectly well that's who I'm talking about."

"Well then, I'm sorry, Mrs. Meade, but I haven't seen him."

The woman grinned back, viciously. "This is private property, you know."

"Not the road, Mrs. Meade. The road ain't private property."

"It sure as hell is! As of ten days ago, it became 'Reynolds Road.' A private road. There are signs." Her grin hardened. "Unless, of course, you're illiterate. Are you illiterate?"

John Marsh put his foot on the clutch, put the truck in gear; "I ain't illiterate," he said evenly, and he executed a K turn on the gravel road, stopped again, and retrieved a sheet of yellow paper from the sun visor. "Mrs. Meade?" he called. The woman looked questioningly at him. She said nothing. "Mrs. Meade?" he repeated.

"Yes?" she said stiffly.

He held the piece of yellow paper out the passenger window, waved it at her. "My name's Marsh. I'm an electrician. I was supposed to do some work for you." He let the paper flutter to the ground. "But I decided just a few minutes ago that I'm all booked up." He touched the accelerator gently and moved slowly away down Reynolds Road.

Dora Meade turned abruptly and disappeared into the tall weeds.

The first three young couples in Granada—The Meades, the McIntyres, the Wentises—were very much of a type, it was true. Bright young suburbanites with a taste for getting ahead, who liked being looked upon as "special," but who tried, to varying degrees, to carry that perception of status with humility. They all gave generously to the proper charities, they all belonged to one of the two major political parties, the men all held white-collar jobs. Which is not to say that these couples were indistinguishable, one from another.

There were, first of all, physical differences. Each of the women was attractive, but in differing ways. Dora Meade was dark, slim, and blatantly sexual; Trudy Wentis, with her penchant for faded blue jeans, and her shoulder-length auburn hair, and her quick, ingratiating smile, looked more like the girl next door; Janice McIntyre appeared friendly, but aloof, a young woman who knew, as if by instinct, what was good and worthy in life, and what was not. Her husband, Miles, for instance, was, she'd say, probably the very best choice she could have made in a husband. He had a quick, inquiring intelligence, as she did; his instincts for the best in life—or at least for the best that was attainable—seemed to match hers; and if he was not as smoothly good-looking as some other men she had known, his angular face and piercing hazel eyes held far more strength and character than those other men, which, after all, she'd say—and believe—counted for much more than mere mannequin-like good looks. Of the three young couples in Granada, the McIntyres' relationship was probably the most secure.

Dora and Larry Meade were in a different boat entirely, and it was a boat that was sinking slowly, though each—for the sake of their son, Timmy—would have denied it. They got married at a very early age, and for the wrong reasons, and now, ten years later, their lives together had become more a matter of staying out of each other's way than anything else: Larry was a tall, lean, and at times exquisitely sensitive man who, Dora had said to her mother, shortly after the marriage began, "is like a big, grinning puppy dog, Mom." His deep sensitivity masked his great inner strength, and since Dora found it difficult—and therefore a waste of her time—to look beyond surface details, she had long since begun to view him as weak-willed, and "maybe" (a suspicion she had also shared with her mother, though much later on) "a trifle disposed toward homosexuality." Larry himself would have smiled easily at the suggestion, though he wouldn't have dismissed it out of hand; he dismissed no idea out of hand; he liked to think that he knew no one very well, especially himself. Life was more interesting that way.

Trudy and Dick Wentis were quite well matched. They respected each other, they joked with each other, their lovemaking—which took up many of their private hours—was filled with "creative kinkiness" (Trudy's phrase) that delighted them both. The child that dwells within all of us dwelt gleefully inside both of them. As did the adult. The only chink in the armor of their relationship was Dick's temper. It seemed to flare most violently when he was trying to cope with Sam, their adopted son. In the past few months, and with the help of a competent psychiatrist, he had come to realize that he was transforming his disappointment with Trudy, because she could not bear children, into anger at Sam, for obvious reasons. Much to Trudy's relief, the relationship between Dick and Sam had improved tremendously, although, she realized, it would probably be years, if ever, before it became a "normal" father-and-son relationship. She looked forward to that day. She thought that when it came she could finally set aside most of the guilt she felt for not being able to have children of her own.

The McIntyres, the Meades, and the Wentises came to Granada in pursuit of a dream. They believed what the brochure had told them about "open spaces and room to breathe—all within the framework of a secure, planned community" because that was what modern living was all about. It was their birthright, wasn't it, to seek out what was most comfortable, and easy.

That was the dream, after all.

And all of them were dreamers.

Part Three
THE ARRIVAL

Chapter 3

The creature had passed this way weeks before, when there had been rain, and wind; the combination had produced a sharp, numbing coldness.

Today, the sun was bright, and warm, and a very slight breeze played sensuously with the fine, light brown hairs on the creature's arms and legs.

The creature was alive.

He had been alive, as well, in the rain and wind, when the numbness had crept over him, and he had felt pain; and a round, aching darkness had formed at the front of his consciousness.

He remembered the pain now, and his muscles tensed as if that time were the present. The darkness—his ignorance of what was happening to him—formed once more.

And almost before it started, almost before the creature had time to realize it had started, it ended.

45

And the warm sunlight and playful, sensuous breezes made his nerves and muscles sing.

He was new to the earth. He had much to learn, much to experience, and very little time to do it before the killing winter came. Thousands had sprung up before him, over the span of half a thousand years. Most had withered and died before a season was through. Those lives and those deaths dwelt within him; if he looked, he would see what those who had gone before had seen, and feel what they felt, and he would find knowledge, and power in that.

But he did not bother to look.

Because, for now, he was being caressed—the earth was caressing him. Just as it had nursed him, and had given him life. And pain. And dizzying pleasure.

The bedroom was large, tastefully decorated. The walls were a very passive, and consequently restful, light green; the two narrow windows—one faced east, the other south—were covered by heavy, cream-colored curtains. The furniture included a king-sized pedestal bed, fashioned from oak, a matching six-drawer chest, a four-drawer chest (the six-drawer's "feminine" counterpart), and an antique cherry wood vanity, with oval mirror. The vanity stood against the east wall, about five feet from the foot of the bed. And Janice McIntyre, naked, stood in front of the vanity. She had placed her right hand gently on her abdomen. She wondered if her husband, Miles—stretched out in expectation on the bed, blankets covering him to the middle of his chest, hands behind his head—had noticed the slight swelling of her abdomen, and, if so, if he had guessed the truth.

"You seem troubled," he said.

Janice grinned slightly, pleased by his unusual sensitivity. Tonight was to be a celebration, unplanned and unverbalized, of their first night in Granada. The celebration had begun with dinner, when she had appeared at the table dressed only in white nylon panties. She sat, leaned forward, studied his plate a moment. "Sir," she said, smiling coyly, "I *do* hope you enjoy the eggplant," which made him laugh, and which, despite their seven years of marriage, had made her blush. The game continued until now, when she pretended to primp, naked, in front of the mirror—for his benefit. But the spirit of the evening, the celebration, was rapidly leaving her; and she noticed a small embarrassment beginning, because his eyes were on her, and he was enjoying her charade. Because, as far as she was concerned, the charade had ended seconds before.

"Yes," she said. "Something's troubling me." She turned, faced him, saw his gaze lower quickly to her right hand—still on her abdomen. She took the hand away and saw his gaze linger on her breasts. She screwed up her mouth a little in annoyance and whispered: "Miles, please–"

"You have a marvelous, lean, and appealing body," he said, as if explaining himself. He grinned boyishly.

"Well, Miles," she began, still at little more than a whisper, "this marvelous, lean, and appealing body is pregnant."

His grin froze. He said nothing for a long moment, and her breathing halted in anticipation. Then—she sighed—his grin broadened: "Janice, that makes me very happy."

She moved slowly, and with much grace, around the foot of the bed to the side. "Thank you, Miles." She leaned over, and with one quick, exquisite movement threw the blankets off the bed.

He put his hands on her hips and gently pulled her onto him: "Thank *you*," he said.

"It's very quiet here, isn't it?" said Norm Gellis, making it clear by his tone that the quiet annoyed him.

His wife, sitting up in bed and reading a romantic novel, said, "But isn't that one of the reasons we came here, Norm?" The question was genuine, but her naturally loud tenor gave it a false edge of sarcasm.

Norm Gellis had been looking out one of their bedroom windows; he stepped back now, and eyed his wife suspiciously. "Tell me something, Marge. Tell me one thing. Tell me what *happens* in the quiet." He paused, although not, she knew, to give her a chance to answer, but because his question, the line of thought he'd latched onto, seemed very ingenious, and he was proud of himself for having come up with it. He stepped back to the window. "I'll tell you what happens in the quiet, Marge. *Nothing* happens in the quiet. Nothing constructive, anyway. Wars don't happen in the quiet, do they? And I'm not talking about that Vietnam thing—that was no war! I'm talking about the good wars. The big wars!" He turned his head and smiled self-importantly at her. "Huh?" he said, his big square head bobbing quickly. "Am I right? Am I right?" He turned back to the window. "And I'll tell you something else, Marge—*progress* don't happen in the quiet, either. Bulldozers and power shovels and jackhammers—they all make shitloads of noise. And you wanta know another thing, Marge? The only thing that *does* happen in the quiet is *rot!* And decay. Yeah." A brief pause for effect. "Rot and decay. That's all!"

"Those are good thoughts," Marge said. She dog-eared a page of the novel to mark her place and put it on an end table near the bed. She smiled at her husband. It was a pleasant gesture, because she was essentially that kind of woman. "Maybe you should go into politics someday." She saw a conspiratorial grin appear on his face.

"Even lovemaking, Marge," he said, his voice a tight, hard whisper. "Even lovemaking."

Marge didn't understand. She stayed quiet.

"Because if you're any kind of man at all you make love like a damned banshee. Know what I mean, Marge?"

Marge said nothing; she was getting a little nervous.

"You shake the goddamned house off its goddamned foundation, Marge! Like a banshee!" He stepped back from the window, put his hand on the ties of his pajama bottoms, worked at them. His gaze was still out the window. "You got yer thing on, Marge? Yer diaphragm? You got that on?"

"Uh-huh," she managed.

Norm Gellis let his pajama bottoms fall. "That's good, Marge." He turned, faced her proudly. " 'Cuz this man here is all set, and nothin' in the world's gonna stand in *his* way!"

*   *   *

"I think we've got an exhibitionist next door," Dora Meade said.

Her husband—inside their walk-in closet, selecting a suit, shirt, tie and shoes for the following morning—called, "What have we got, Dora?"

She kept her eyes on the lighted window a hundred feet away. "An exhibitionist," she repeated, though only a smidgen louder. "An *exhibitionist!*"

Her husband, dressed in a crisp, white T-shirt and jockey shorts, appeared from the closet. He was a tall, well-muscled man with dark, receding hair, unusually large, dark eyes, a small nose, and a general air of bemusement and sensitivity about him that Dora Meade had, years before, found appealing. Now, she thought, it was merely annoying and childish. "I'm sorry, Dora," he said. "You're going to have to repeat yourself. I really couldn't—"

"I *said* that the guy next door—What's his name? Gellis?—I said he was exhibiting himself in his bedroom window."

Larry Meade came over and stood by the window with her. He peered out. After a moment, he said, "I can't see a thing, Dora."

She shouldered him away from the window. "Well of course you can't. He turned the damned light off."

"Oh." Larry went to his twin bed, checked the alarm clock. "Don't let me oversleep in the morning, Dora. That appointment tomorrow is super critical . . ."

"I don't *believe* you," Dora cut in. "I really do not believe you! There's some guy next door who gets his kicks out of showing his cock off to any female eyes within sight of it, and all you can say is, 'Don't let me oversleep'?!"

Larry sat heavily on the bed; he looked apologetically up at his wife. "It was probably some kind of accident, Dora."

She laughed suddenly, sarcastically, the kind of hard and unamused guffaw he heard from her once or twice a day. He thought, now, that it was beginning to bother him.

"You can't be serious, Larry. Do you actually want me to believe that that man's pants fell down accidentally! I suppose his erection was an accident, too. Is that what you're going to tell me?"

"Isn't it kind of a long distance to tell if he had an erection or not?" Larry said, smiling uneasily.

Dora stared incredulously at him for a long moment. Then she went to her bed, climbed under the blankets, and turned off the bedside lamp.

Chapter 4

The creature very tentatively put his fingers to the wall, as if the wall might be hot, or cold, or as if it might be an enemy of some kind. This was the first time he had entered one of the houses, and he sensed hostility—a kind of deep and unnatural tension.

He found the wall warm, and smooth, and hard. Like live skin over flat bone. He disliked the feel of it and he pulled his hand away.

He moved very slowly about the dark room, his gaze passing quickly from here to there, uncomprehending. He was new to the earth and most of what he saw he had no choice but to accept without question.

But, like the walls of the room, the room itself and its furnishings made him feel strangely out of place and, suddenly, his usually slow, deep, and even breathing became erratic, as if the air were being forced from his lungs, as if, somehow, the house itself wanted to take his life from him.

And then—although he was unable to verbalize it—he knew that, in this house, within these walls, *he* was the enemy. Because he had sensed the other living things in the house, had sensed their fear quivering deep inside them, like a rabbit quivers deep in its burrow.

That fear gave the creature incredible strength and courage. It excited him, made his muscles tense.

He stopped very briefly at the bottom of the stairway.

And something which might, in a human being, pass for longing, or hunger, settled into his huge, exquisite, pale blue eyes.

And then he started up the stairs.

It probably was better here than in the city, like his father had told him, Timmy Meade decided. Sure, there were people in the city (like Tony and Sheila and Mike) that he probably wouldn't see ever again, but there were kids here he could be friends with, too. Sam Wentis, for instance, who was a little strange, sure, but that was okay. And besides, it wasn't as if this was the first move of his life; it probably wouldn't be the last, either. So, he knew what the word "adjustment" meant. He even thought he was pretty grown up to "adjust" as well as he had. But, damn (it was the only curse his parents allowed him), he really would miss Tony and Mike. And especially Sheila.

He rolled to his back. Sam Wentis, he thought, wasn't just a little strange, he was a lot strange. He had a screw loose somewhere, he wasn't playing with a full deck, he had toys in his attic. Why else would he try to walk across the damn swamp on

the other side of the woods (and almost drown in
the damn smelly green water while he was at it),
and why else would he go chasing a damn raccoon
all over the place, grunting all the while like some
damn pig? That wasn't funny. That was just dumb.
It was no wonder the raccoon bit him.

Timmy Meade let his eyes open. He realized,
suddenly, that it would be a long time before he
adjusted completely to this place. Losing old friends,
getting new ones—that was pretty easy (not real
easy, not like fallin' off a log, for sure, but easy
enough). Getting adjusted to a new place, though,
was something else again. He wasn't certain why.
Maybe, he considered, it was because the *place*
was always there, always around him. Like a new
skin. When snakes got their new skins, they probably itched for a while until they got used to them.
Timmy Meade thought that that was what he was
doing now. Itching. Because this new place scared
him a little. Uh-uh, he corrected himself immediately. Not scared, really. Just itchy uncomfortable.
Because in the city, there was always something
going on—car horns blasting, people talking loudly
in the next apartment, sirens of one kind or another
blaring away, jets going over. And it was funny,
but while he was living there, in the city, he'd
never really noticed those noises, and all the others. He supposed now that somebody could have
said to him, "Hey, you lying there in that city bed,
tell me what you hear," and he would have said, "I
don't hear nothin'." And it would have been the
truth. Because the loud talking, and the horns
blasting, and the sirens blaring were all a *part* of
the *place*.

And, he realized at last, that it was their absence, the silence here, that was making him itchy uncomfortable.

Tense, he thought suddenly. He was feeling tense. As if, while he was lying here in the dark and the quiet, in this new place, something waited very, very patiently—something that was a *part* of *this* place, and had been a part of it for years and years—like the big, gnarled oak tree close to the main gates.

"Damn!" he whispered, angry that he could so easily frighten himself.

He pushed himself up to a sitting position. He inhaled deeply. He reached to his right and switched on the bedside lamp.

He grinned, relieved.

The room was empty.

The house was quiet.

Chapter 5

Marge Gellis gave Deputy Sheriff Peters the cup of coffee he'd asked for; she noticed her hands were trembling, that some of the coffee had spilled over onto the saucer. "Oh," she said, "I'm sorry." She noticed her voice was trembling, too. "I'll get you another cup."

"No," the deputy said, "this is fine—"

Norm Gellis hunched over on the couch, hands folded in front of him (like his wife, he had put a robe on over his pajamas), cut in, "Marge, go back downstairs. You're not gonna be any good to no one the way you are."

"I'd rather she stayed," said the deputy.

Norm Gellis looked up at him, surprised. "She didn't see nothin', *Sheriff!*" He nearly spat the word.

"I'd rather she stayed," the deputy repeated. He was a short, dark, and very solidly built man in his

57

early forties; it was clear from his tone and manner that he was accustomed to obedience. "It happens, Mr. Gellis, that people sometimes don't know for certain what they've seen until after the shock wears off and they've had a chance to calm down. Do you understand that?"

Norm Gellis shrugged as if the entire matter had suddenly become distasteful to him. "Hey, if she wants to stay . . ."

"Thank you," said the deputy. He seated himself in a La-Z-Boy opposite the couch and leaned forward. "How old would you say the child was, Mr. Gellis?"

"I told you before—"

"Please tell me again."

Norm rolled his eyes. "About ten—he was about ten. Eleven, maybe."

"About ten or eleven. And you say he was dark-skinned; could he have been black?"

"I don't think so."

"You don't think so?"

"It was hard to tell. The room was dark."

"Would you say the boy was white?"

"Yeah, sure." A short pause. "He was white."

"Can you be certain of that, Mr. Gellis?"

"I don't know. He could have been a damned spick, for God's sake!"

"Sorry? I don't understand."

"A Puerto Rican, a spick, Sheriff. You comprehende?" He chuckled.

"Do you believe he was Puerto Rican, Mr. Gellis?"

"Christ, no—I was only joking!"

"Oh?" The hint of a smile appeared and disappeared quickly on the deputy's lips. He turned his head and addressed Marge Gellis. "Can you add anything to what your husband has told me, Mrs. Gellis?"

Marge, standing a few feet to the left of the couch, looked suddenly ill at ease. She said nothing for a long moment, then, "I really didn't get a very good . . . look at him."

The deputy quickly turned his entire body toward her. "Just tell me what you saw, Mrs. Gellis. Just let it come back to you slowly—I think you'll be surprised at . . ."

"He wasn't black," Marge cut in. "I know he wasn't black."

"But your husband said the room was dark, Mrs. Gellis."

"I thought you didn't see nothin', Marge!" There was anger in Norm Gellis's tone. "You told me—"

"Mr. Gellis, please, I've explained—"

And Marge interrupted, "He was running from me, toward the top of the stairs, and there was a light on in the bathroom . . ." She stopped, remembered. "And I could see his face pretty clearly, just for a second, less than a second, really." A short pause, then, "And I saw his . . . eyes, his expression—" She stopped; she seemed suddenly confused. Her gaze fell slowly from the deputy's face to her hands, clasped tightly in front of her. Her confusion grew harder, more obvious. "My God," she murmured. "My God!"

"Mrs. Gellis, are you all right?"

"My God!" She looked up. The confusion was gone—a stark and knowing fear had replaced it. "Sheriff, he . . . that boy, I mean, he . . ."

The deputy stood quickly, went to her, put his arms around her shoulders to steady her. "Come over here, Mrs. Gellis." He coaxed her gently to

the La-Z-Boy and helped her into it. She sat with
her hands flat on the arms of the chair, her head
down.

The deputy knelt on one knee beside the chair.
He put his hand on her hand and spoke softly,
reassuringly. "Now, Mrs. Gellis, I want you to take
a few deep breaths ..." He paused, hoped for
some response, got none. "A few deep breaths,
Mrs. Gellis. You're obviously in some kind of shock—"
She lifted her head suddenly. Turned it. Looked
him squarely in the eye. "Mrs. Gellis?" he said.
Her look unnerved him. The fear had vanished;
now great relief was obvious around her eyes and
mouth. "Mrs. Gellis, do you have something you'd
like to add to what you've already told me?"

She answered quickly, "Norm's right."

"I don't understand, Mrs. Gellis."

"I said Norm's right. I didn't see *any*thing."

The deputy heard Norm Gellis change position
on the couch. He turned his head and looked at
him. Norm was smiling oddly. The deputy turned
back to Marge. "The boy was running *away* from
you," he began, in an attempt to coax her, "and in
the light from the bathroom, you say you—"

"I'm sorry," she cut in, "but I can't tell you a
thing. I really can't."

Deputy Peters studied her face. He saw that she
actually believed what she was telling him now. At
last, and reluctantly, he said, "Yes. Forgive me."
He stood, took a small, Sony cassette recorder from
a pocket on his belt. "Mr. Gellis," he began, "I'd
like you to repeat everything you've told me, for
the record, please."

Norm Gellis said, "No, I don't think so. It was
her idea"—he nodded quickly at his wife, as if

embarrassed—"to call you in the first place. And the more I think about it, the more I think I shouldn'ta gone along with her. It ain't real important, is it? I can handle it. Just some goddamned kid playin' around, and if he comes back, I'll take care of him." He smiled again; the deputy saw hostility in that smile and he wondered at whom it was directed, exactly. "I'll take *good* care of him, don't you worry."

The deputy put the tape recorder back on his belt. "You know, Mr. Gellis, that the laws regarding trespass do not allow—"

"I know all about the law, Sheriff." He paused for effect. "And so will that boy if he ever shows up here again." He nodded at the door. "Thanks for coming by, Sheriff."

John Marsh stopped the pickup truck just to the left of the big, ornate, black iron gate. The word GRANADA, done in what looked, in the glare of the headlights, like stainless steel, stretched across the gate; GRAN on the left side, ADA on the right. He had noted the other signs weeks ago—crisp, black capital letters on large, white, rectangular backgrounds, spaced like Burma Shave signs down the length of the road: REYNOLDS ROAD. PRIVATE PROPERTY. KEEP OUT. NO UNAUTHORIZED PERSONS OR VEHICLES ALLOWED. He supposed now that he should not have come here again. But, for the first time in a decade, he was very drunk. And when he got drunk he got especially nostalgic and sloppy. And when that happened, he did foolish things—which was why, he considered, he so rarely got drunk.

"Granada," he mumbled, "Granada," he repeated, as if the word were a ball of phlegm he'd

managed to cough up. And then he did start to
cough in earnest—a liquid, gurgling kind of cough.
The very sound of it made him queasy. The cough-
ing continued for several minutes, then it stopped
abruptly. And he realized that Matt Peters was
tapping on the driver's window.

Marsh grinned stupidly and rolled the window
down. "Hello, Matt. Whatcha doin'? You tuckin'
these people in?"

"John, do you have business here?"

"At this hour of the damned morning? Shit no."

"Then do you mind telling me . . ." The deputy
paused a moment. "Are you *drunk*, John?"

"Uh-huh. Sick, too. You got some Bromo?" he
chuckled softly. "I could really use some Bromo."

"Christ, John, I wish you hadn't done this! We've
got special orders from the sheriff himself about
this place—"

"*Shit* on this place, Matt!"

The deputy put his hand on the door handle.
"You're going to have to come back with me, John.
I'll drop you at your place—"

"You like what they're doin' here, Matt?" Marsh
nodded in the general direction of the iron gate.
"You really like what they're doin' here?"

Deputy Peters opened the door slowly. "I haven't
given it a lot of thought, John. Now do you want to
climb out of that truck, please."

"You don't remember the Griffins, do you, Matt?"

"No, John, I don't. That was before my time.
Now I'm going to have to insist that you get out of
the truck. I've got a report to file, and I'm very
tired—"

"Real . . . fine people, Matt." He was beginning
to slur his words badly; the deputy had trouble

understanding him. "Stupid, foolish ... people, for sure, but fine people, too, and they had fine dreams, Matt."

The deputy shook his head slowly. "John, will you please–"

And John Marsh fell very heavily and quickly from the driver's seat to the road. He lay face down, vomit trickling from his mouth. The deputy leaned over, rolled him to his side. "Christ, John!" With great effort he pulled and prodded and pushed the man to a sitting position against the driver's door. "John, are you all right?"

A slight, sad grin appeared on Marsh's face. He burped several times in quick succession, then put his hand on his stomach. "Yeah," he said finally. "Yeah, I'm okay." He nodded slightly to indicate the iron gate and the massive, dark shapes of the houses—many were still in various stages of construction—beyond it. He saw a light wink on in one of the houses. "I'm fine," he repeated. A half mile west of the farthest houses, the small, deciduous forest was silhouetted against a pale sky. Directly overhead, a few of the brighter stars still were visible. "But I'll tell you something, Matt." His voice was steady now. "Kind of a secret— between you and me, I mean."

"John, why don't you just try standing up. I'll give you a lift home and tomorrow we can–"

" 'Cuz I been comin' here from time to time in the last couple weeks, Matt, and I been seein' things, and I wanta share this secret with you. I wanta tell you that these people here, behind that godawful fence, in those goddamn houses, Matt–" He closed his eyes briefly, as if in pain. "These people *ain't* all right, Matt. I don't know why, for sure, not for sure." He pressed his hand hard into his stomach. He grinned again. "But I know this, Matt—I know they're gonna learn to regret ever comin' here. I know that for a fact. And if there was somethin' I could do about it, I would. But I can't."

And he passed into unconsciousness.

Fifteen Years Earlier

It was all much better now, Rachel Griffin told herself.

She leaned against the living room doorway and folded her arms across her stomach. It hadn't taken much, she thought, to make it better—just a few odds and ends of furniture: a white wicker chair, hers; a red winged-back chair, Paul's; a small cherry wood table; a rolltop writing desk, very old; a brightly colored rug; and, more importantly, plans to erase the awful damage done to the house. That wasn't much. In time it would be quite a beautiful little house. One day, she might even be able to call it home.

She felt something tickling her ankle. She looked. "Hello, cat," she said. She'd have to think of a name for the animal, of course. She couldn't go on calling it "cat," although Paul seemed to feel it was all that was required. "It's not like it's a bona fide member of the family," he'd told her. "It's just a cat, and it's supposed to be quite a mouser. God knows this house needs one."

She stroked the cat, pleased by the upward-thrusting motions of its huge gray head. "I don't care what Paul says," she cooed. "You're going to have a name, like everyone else."

Chapter 6

October 1

"When's fall start?" Sam Wentis asked.

"I don't know," Timmy Meade answered. "I guess whenever it's good and ready to start—when it gets colder, I guess."

"Naw, my mom says it starts in September sometime," Sam Wentis said, and he pointed suddenly, enthusiastically, to the middle of an acre-size, malodorous swamp they'd just come upon. "Hey, looka that! Turtle stuck his nose right up outa the water! You see that!?"

Timmy Meade looked quizzically at him. "Big deal," he said. "How are they gonna breathe unless they stick their noses up outa the water?"

"I *know* that," Sam Wentis said. "What're you sayin'? You sayin' I think turtles are fish or somethin'? I know a lot about turtles."

Timmy Meade raised his head and rolled his eyes. He wondered if he would ever figure Sam

Wentis out. "No, Sam, I'm not sayin' that. I know you know about turtles. Everyone knows about turtles."

"Sure as hell!" said Sam Wentis, and he smirked a little, proud of his curse.

"Damn it to hell!" said Timmy Meade, and he turned away so his friend wouldn't see his broad smile and know the truth—that he was trying to best him in cursing.

"Shit damn it all to hell and back!" exclaimed Sam Wentis, and both of them burst into loud, nervous, adolescent laughter. The laughter lasted nearly five minutes, then, like a spinning top, slowly subsided and finally stopped. Timmy Meade said, "Hey, let's get outa here. It smells like shit damn rotten eggs." And, after some thought, Sam Wentis agreed that the swamp really did smell like "shit damn rotten eggs, now that you mention it." So, Timmy checked his new watch—an eleventh birthday gift—decided, after consultation with Sam, that they had a good hour left before dinner, and, side by side, they headed north, into a particularly dark, thick, and very intriguing area of the woods.

Sam Wentis and Timmy Meade had become inseparable in the ten weeks they'd lived in Granada. As much as any two boys can be they were an amazing study in contrasts: Sam was tall, dark-haired, olive-skinned. His adoptive mother was fond of saying he had a "decidedly Mediterranean look about him," and her friends invariably commented that "the girls are going to be falling all over him," and, "He's going to be a real lady's man," which, for reasons she couldn't understand, made Trudy Wentis very uncomfortable. And Sam was also "impetuous," which, his parents realized, might have been a euphemism for "bullheaded" and "slow," although the second word was never used in the Wentis household, because it was agreed that perhaps Sam wasn't really "slow" so much as "contemplative," in his own unique way.

Timmy Meade, on the other hand, was short, fair-skinned, and fair-haired, with the kind of "thoughtful good looks" which, later in his life (his father maintained) only a few, especially sensitive women would find appealing. And he was extremely bright. His mother often wished that IQ testing hadn't fallen into general disuse. She was sure that her son's score would really be something to brag about. She was that kind of woman.

" 'Round the end of September, sometime," Sam Wentis said.

Timmy Meade didn't understand. "What's around the end of September, Sam?"

Sam Wentis put his open hand against the trunk of a tree. "That's when fall starts. I just remembered." He noticed the long thorns spaced randomly on the tree. "Hey, Timmy, looka this!" He took his hand away and fingered one of the thorns, fascinated. "Jees—you could really get speared by one of these things." He pushed his finger deliberately into the tip of the thorn and watched, still fascinated, as a small bead of blood formed. "Jees, these things could kill ya."

"That was a dumb thing to do," Timmy Meade said. "How do you know it's not poisonous? You could be rolling around on the ground there in a couple minutes." He nodded meaningfully at the ground. "Then you could be *dead!* Shit damn!

That was dumb! Dumbest thing I've seen you do all week! Why do you do things like that?"

Sam Wentis said nothing. He brought his finger slowly to his mouth and licked the blood off. Then, abruptly, he turned and started walking north. Timmy Meade lowered his head; *Jees, not again!*? He looked up. "Sam," he called, "I didn't mean nothin'. Really." But Sam Wentis kept walking; he quickened his pace a little. Timmy Meade stayed where he was; he had decided, at that moment, that his friend's temper wasn't going to get the best of him *this* time: It seemed like every day he had to apologize to him for saying one thing or another. Yesterday, it had been the thing with the garbage cans ("Sam, why would you wanta go pokin' around in someone else's garbage? You could catch a disease." . . . "I'm sorry, Sam. I didn't mean nothin'."). And the day before that it had been the thing with the puppy ("Sam, don't do that, can't you see yer hurtin' him?" . . . "I'm sorry, Sam."), because Sam couldn't seem to understand that some of the things he did made no sense at all. Or that they were stupid and cruel things.

"I'm not going to apologize this time, Sam," Timmy Meade called. "I don't think I need to, 'cuz if you just think about it a little, Sam, you'll *know* you did a dumb thing!" He paused. And realized, on the instant, that Sam had vanished. A nervous smile played along his lips. "Sam?" He looked quickly to his right, his left. Then at the spot where Sam had last been. "Sam, you hidin' behind a tree?" He paused very briefly. "You behind a tree or somethin', Sam?" From far to his left—to the west—he heard the crack of a rifle. He turned his head toward the sound; the phrase *hunting season* passed through his mind and made him grimace. He turned his head back, focused on the spot where Sam had been. And saw him standing, facing him, smiling an odd, crooked kind of smile. "Shit damn!" Sam Wentis said, and he looked very pleased, as if he had just won some great victory. "Shit damn!" he repeated.

Clyde Watkins and Manny Kent: Townies

Clyde Watkins called, "What'd you shoot at, Manny?"

Manny Kent ("Manny" was short for "Manfred," which he despised) looked up from the deer spoor. "Damn buck," he called back. "Didn'tcha see it? Great big damned buck, Clyde. Mighta got him, too, weren't the sun in my eyes."

Clyde walked over to him, very careful of how he carried his rifle (the year before, Clyde's Uncle Winston had accidentally shot himself in the chin. Miraculously, he had survived but, Clyde thought now, he'd never again be much to look at). "I didn't see a thing, Manny. You got X-ray vision or somethin'?"

"Naw, I ain't got X-ray vision. Yer just blind, Clyde." He laughed. "Blind's a bat in a snowstorm, Clyde."

Clyde nodded to indicate the deer spoor. "That ain't no deer spoor, Manny." It lay on a slight rise in the land: To the east, the land sloped downward at a gentle angle for several hundred yards, where a newly installed, six-foot-high chain-link fence bisected it. Just beyond the fence, the land gave way to heavy thickets and small stands of ever-

greens. Granada lay three-quarters of a mile east of
the fence.

"Sure that's a deer spoor, Clyde. You gonna tell
me I shot at some damn cow?"

"That ain't a deer spoor at all, Manny." He paused,
suppressed a giggle. "That's a Steg-oh-saurus spoor.
And it's a very rare thing, Manny."

Manny eyed him suspiciously. "That's a *what*,
Clyde?"

"A Steg-oh-saurus spoor." He felt the laughter
building in his stomach, like a whirlpool; he fought
it back. "You ain't hearda the *Steg*-oh-saurus?"

"You jokin' with me, Clyde?"

"I ain't jokin' with you, Manny. That's an actual
Steg-oh-saurus spoor, there. It *looks* like a deer
spoor, but it ain't." He paused, grinned. "Woulda
fooled me, too, if I didn't know the difference. It's a
real subtle difference, Manny."

"Yer fulla shit, Clyde, 'cuz I *know* what a Steg-
oh-lasoris is! It's some kinda fuckin' dinosaur, some
kinda fuckin' damn big dinosaur, and yer tryin' to
make *me* look like a damn fool! Admit it, Clyde. Go
on, admit it." There was no animosity in Manny's
tone; he'd grown accustomed to his brother-in-law's
off-key sense of humor, and it made him feel good
when one of Clyde's jokes fell flat. "Go on, Clyde,
admit it."

"Yeah, you're right," Clyde said, as if in apology.
"But it ain't no dinosaur, Manny." Again he suppressed a giggle. "It's actually a kind of wild *pig*!"
And then the whirlpool of laughter burst from his
mouth, he dropped his rifle, fell to his knees and,
the laughter frothing out of him, enjoyed himself
immensely.

Minutes later, when he could open his eyes again,

when, at last, the laughter had died, he saw that Manny was holding something in front of his— Clyde's—eyes; a small, rectangular piece of tarnished metal; a badly rusted chain hung from it. "What's that, Manny?"

Manny held it up to his own eyes, and studied it critically; "I think it's somebody's bracelet, Clyde. And I think it's made of pure silver."

Clyde stood and picked his rifle up; he examined the bracelet closely, while Manny clung possessively to it, then he announced, "Sure looks like pure silver, Manny." He tried to take it from him; Manny yanked it away. "Finders are keepers, Clyde." He nodded at what appeared to be a broad, flat, dull white rock, half buried in the bare earth, about a yard away. "*I* found it. Over there, under that rock. I saw the chain stickin' out."

"Well let me tell you this, Manny. If it is silver, you just remember that it was *my* pickup that brought you out here, and *my* thirty-ought-thirty yer huntin' with, and *my* damned boots yer wearing–"

"There's a name on it, Clyde."

"You listenin' to me, Manny?"

"Ever hearda someone named Mark Collins, Clyde?—'Cuz that's the name here: 'Mark Collins.' "

Clyde thought for just a moment; then, "Give it here, Manny."

"I sure as hell will not!"

"It's evidence, Manny."

"Evidence? What kind of evidence?" He sounded on the verge of a pout.

"You're thick, Manny! You got no brains, nor memory! Mark Collins was that colored man who disappeared around here six or seven years ago.

You remember?! It was in the papers, and I know you can read."

Something close to recognition settled into Manny's eyes; "Oh yeah," he said.

"So give me the damned bracelet, Manny, 'cuz it ain't yours, anyway, 'cuz first of all it's evidence, and second of all–" He stopped, annoyed. Manny had stepped away from him and was prodding the dull white rock with the toe of his boot. "Clyde . . ." he said tentatively.

Clyde stepped over to him, hesitated a moment, then leaned over and pushed him away. For a long while he studied and fingered what they had supposed was a rock, then he looked up at his brother-in-law. "Give me the bracelet, Manny!"

Manny obeyed instantly. Clyde's tone had become severe, even threatening.

"Manny, this here ain't no rock. It's a pelvic bone." He wiped the bracelet clean with his handkerchief.

"It's a *what*, Clyde?"

"A pelvic bone. From somebody's *pelvis*, from *Mark Collins's* pelvis." He tucked the bracelet under the bone, back where Manny had found it.

"Clyde, what would you know about bones?"

"I'm the volunteer fire chief, right, Manny?! And as a consequence of that I seen lotsa bones. I seen skull bones and I seen wristbones and backbones, and I seen pelvic bones, too. And this here is a pelvic bone. And I'll tell you somethin' else, Manny, somethin' I hope makes you real sick, 'cuz I don't wanta know about this man here, or what's left of him, and I don't wanta know we found him, and I'm real upset that *you* found him, so I want you to be sick when I tell you that someone's been *gnawin'* on this pelvic bone here! I don't know what's been gnawin' on it—a coyote or a bobcat, maybe. Maybe not. But somethin'. And I'm gonna tell you one more thing, Manny"—he started for the car at a fast walk; Manny followed—"I'm gonna tell you," Clyde shouted over his shoulder, "that if you ever so much as mention one word to *any*one about this, about what we found out here, even if you mention it to that skinny little wife of yers–"

"Clyde, she's *yer* sister!"

"Even to her, Manny, then your ass is grass and *I'm* the mower. I'm tellin' you that right now, and I'll tell you again tomorrow, and the next day, 'cuz I don't want *no* part of somebody's fuckin' murder, you hear that, Manny, no part, no way, and you better remember–"

Timmy Meade asked, "Think you'd ever come out here at night, Sam?"

Sam Wentis considered the question a moment. "Sure," he said, with conviction. "Ain't nothin' here at night that's not here in the day. My father told me that and I guess it's true."

Timmy Meade smiled to himself; Sam Wentis so rarely talked about his adoptive parents. "Is that what your father said? Sounds real good to me."

"But I knew it all along, anyway."

"I know you did, Sam."

" 'Course, there's things out here in the day you got to be real careful of."

"Yeah, I know, Sam. I heard there's timber rattlers, and maybe some brown bears . . ."

In unison, they stopped walking. They had reached the edge of the forest—above them, the full and overhanging branches of two beech trees side by side formed a perfect, natural archway. From here, they had a grand, panoramic view of Granada, a half mile off, bathed in the dull, orange glow of sunset.

"My dad told me we'll probably all get stuck out here this winter," Timmy Meade said. "Because the road's too narrow and they'd better widen it. But, heck, I hope they don't widen it. Just think of all the days we'll have off from school, Sam." He waited for some response but got none. "Sam?"

And, after a moment, Sam Wentis whispered, "Shit damn!" He repeated it once, louder. Then again, even louder. And then he took off at a loping and impossibly graceful run toward Granada. He had always been a very graceful and quick child.

Chapter 7

With the tips of her fingers, Janice McIntyre gently traced the slight swelling at her abdomen. She thought, *Hello little one*; it made her feel suddenly foolish. She hoped Miles wouldn't wake, see that she wasn't in bed, and come looking for her. Sure, he'd be able to understand that "pregnant women need their special, private moments, Miles," but maybe he'd think there was something wrong, something she wasn't telling him, and wouldn't she really rather he stayed and talked with her a while? But, she considered, his day had been long and wearisome—he'd probably sleep well past the alarm.

She seated herself at the breakfast nook; she reached to her left for the light switch and decided, no, the near-darkness was better (Miles had installed a spotlight on the back of the house, just outside the big kitchen window—"For security purposes, Janice"—and most of the backyard was bathed now in its soft yellow glow). She imagined she did her best thinking in the dark. She remembered that her decision to marry Miles—eight years before—had come to her at 2 A.M., in her darkened Utica, New York, studio apartment. And her decision to forget her job as a high school art teacher and to devote herself entirely to Jodie had come to her in the darkness and quiet of the hospital's labor room, just an hour and a half before Jodie's birth.

She touched her abdomen again and thought, very briefly (not for the first time) of reincarnation— that, perhaps, it was Jodie growing inside her. Again. And she pushed the thought away because— as she had decided before—it was stupid. And unfair.

Her gaze settled on the big, open, beautifully manicured backyard, on the white marble birdbath, and the four flowering dogwood trees they'd planted, essentially at random, and the little, barntype tool shed just at the edge of the yard. She thought, as she let her gaze wander idly from here to there, that this would be a very good place indeed to bring up any child.

And then, almost against her will, her eyes stopped moving, and her gaze settled on a spot just inside the perimeter of the light, a couple yards to the left of the tool shed—where the illumination was weakest—and she said, just below a whisper, "Who's that?"

A woman was standing there; tall, dark-haired, pretty. And she was standing very still. . . .

When he was a child, John Marsh often woke very early in the morning (as he had this morning) and a special kind of nervous, sweaty fear had prodded at him. *Go on, open your eyes, I dare you; open them!* And he remembered, now, that he had never been able to keep his eyes closed, convinced though he was that something hugely grotesque waited for him, something designed to take his senses away and reduce him to jelly. He realized now that that kind of fear had settled over him again, after nearly a fifty-year absence, but that this time there was reason for it. And he remembered, suddenly, that he had awakened this way the night before, and the night before that—Remembered that for the past ten nights, ever since his stupid, drunken drive to Granada, he had awakened early, convinced that *she* had followed him back.

She? he wondered, and knew immediately that it was a way of denying, futilely, what had happened.

He swung his feet off the bed to the floor. He switched a light on and quickly scanned his small, memorabilia-filled bedroom. He saw no one. He told himself that he knew he wouldn't. The room had been empty last night, and the night before, and the night before that. And, he knew, it would stay empty. Because Rachel Griffin would have no reason at all to follow him. She was where she wanted to be. Where eternity wanted to keep her. Where her husband and her poor handful of dreams were.

Then, as it had for the past ten nights, the moment came back to him, replayed itself.

She said nothing. She smiled a sad, pretty smile, and reached for him through the closed driver's window. She touched his face. And he remembered now that, yes, her touch had been very cold.

Deathly cold. But she hadn't—he knew even then— been trying to give him her coldness. She had been saying hello. To an old friend. One she hadn't seen for a decade and a half.

Janice McIntyre was glad her husband had come downstairs. She wasn't sure why. Maybe, she thought, her mood had changed. Maybe being alone, and in the dark, here, in this particular house, was going to take some getting used to.

Miles turned the bright overhead light on; he seated himself across from her at the breakfast nook, and asked if she'd like some coffee or some cocoa. She said no. He reached across the small table and took her hand; "Is something wrong, Jan?"

"Nothing's wrong," she said. "We pregnant women just need our private moments."

"Yes," he said, and paused. "But are you sure . . ."

"I'm sure." She squeezed his hand to reassure him. "Nothing's wrong."

"Okay," he said, though he sounded unconvinced. He stood. "I'm going to make myself some cocoa, anyway."

"Miles?"

"Yes?" He went to a cupboard, opened it.

"Who lives next door, Miles?" She nodded out the kitchen window. "Don't the Gellises live there? Isn't that their name? Gellis?"

Miles found the cocoa and went to the stove with it. "Uh-huh. I've said, let me see—" He feigned remembering. "Exactly eight words to them." He grinned, took a teapot off the stove, filled it at the sink.

"Is she tall, Miles? Mrs. Gellis, I mean. Is she tall? And does she have long, dark hair—"

Miles glanced at her incredulously. "Are you kidding, Jan? You've seen her, you were introduced to her, in fact, and she's just the opposite–"

"Oh. Yes. Well, I was only wondering. I saw this woman out there"—she nodded at the window—"and I thought that at this hour of the morning–"

Miles cut in, "There's something I need to tell you, Jan."

"Yes?" she said, annoyed by his interruption.

He mixed the cocoa and hot water, brought it back to the table. "Mr. Jenner called me at the office, today–"

"The real estate agent?"

"Uh-huh. He wanted to talk about that . . . thing–" He paused. "About the child they found here–"

"I don't want to hear this, Miles. I really do not–"

"Janice, I think it's way past time that you accepted Jodie's death! *Five* years, Janice, almost six–" He stopped. A cold, expressionless anger had come into Janice's face, had transformed it.

"I know he's dead, Miles." She said the words in a strange, quiet monotone, her lips barely moving. "If you'll remember, if you'll take the time to remember, *I* was the one who found him, and *I* was the one who tried . . . to breathe life back into him–" She began to weep.

"Jan, this is pointless. It's not Jodie we're discussing, for Christ's sake. We're discussing some poor, dead child neither of us ever knew. And I wanted to tell you that Jenner said the D.A. in Penn Yann isn't going to involve us in any investigation. He feels . . ." Miles paused; Janice had stopped weeping. The anger remained, but it was slowly dissipating. "The District Attorney seems to feel," Miles repeated, his tone softer, "that the Griffins were somehow responsible. Apparently, when the Griffins lived here, there were lots of rumors–"

"The Griffins?" Janice cut in.

"Yes, Jan. I've told you about them; their house stood almost precisely on the spot where this one stands now."

"Oh yes," Janice said; she remembered obliquely that it was something he'd told her weeks ago. "Yes," she repeated. The anger had all but vanished, now—only traces remained, as if she had come in from a frigid winter night and hadn't quite finished warming herself.

"And the D.A. says the child was probably their responsibility–"

"Miles, you've told me what you wanted to tell me." Her tone was crisp. "So, if you don't mind, can we please just drop it?"

Miles looked silently at her for a moment; then, "Yes. I'm sorry. Let's go to bed."

"You've barely touched your cocoa, Miles. Finish it. Then we'll go to bed." She smiled a tentative, apologetic smile. He smiled back immediately.

She said, "Melissa."

" 'Melissa'?"

"If it's a girl, Miles, we'll name her Melissa. And Francis if it's a boy. What do you think?"

"Can we talk about it?" he said, grinning.

"Sure we can talk about it. Make me a cup of cocoa and we'll talk."

Fifteen Years Earlier

Nothing marked the spot—no crudely improvised cross, no stone. All Rachel knew, as she looked out their bedroom window, her hand holding the heavy curtain aside, was that the boy had been buried "north of the house." Although she had—uncertain why—asked Paul to show her the exact spot, he had merely reiterated "north of the house," and added that it was all she needed to know. She realized that she was grateful he'd been so close-mouthed. If she'd been with him at the burial and knew the spot she would probably have gone to it daily, perhaps to mutter "I'm sorry!" over and over again, as she had done before, or perhaps merely to remember, and to regret. This way, she could almost convince herself that the boy hadn't been buried at all. That, in fact, he hadn't even died.

Chapter 8

Norm Gellis opened the door wide, took a bag of groceries from his wife, and peered into it. "Did you get 'em, Marge?"

"Yes, Norm, I did. Two boxes, like you said."

"Are they the right size, Marge? You didn't get the wrong size, did you?"

"Whatever you added to the list, Norm." She made her way into the kitchen. "I didn't even look at it," she called back. "I just gave it to the man behind the counter."

Norm followed her into the kitchen and set the bag down on the table. "Okay, so where are they? —In that bag, there?" He nodded at the bag Marge still carried. She set it on the table.

"I don't know, Norm." She sounded vaguely annoyed. "They're here somewhere."

He grinned at her. "Does this bother you, Marge? Does it make you a little queasy?"

She retrieved a box of Sugar Pops from one of the bags, turned her back to him, put the box in a cupboard. "It doesn't bother me, Norm. Like you said, we need to protect ourselves."

"I know that's what I said, Marge. But do you believe it?"

She turned, smiled. *I'm on your side,* the smile said. "Of course I believe it, Norm."

"Damn right!" He took some cans out of one of the bags. "Who in the fuck packed these, Marge? Did you pack 'em?" He withdrew a box of Charter Arms hollow-point .38 calibre bullets from the bottom of the bag; he studied the box closely for a moment; he opened it, withdrew one of the slugs, and held it up lengthwise, between his thumb and forefinger, at half an arm's length, so his wife could see it. "It don't really look like much, does it, Marge?"

She hesitated, then, "It's not supposed to look like much, is it?"

He grinned again. "It'll take most of your head clean off, Marge. Did you know that?"

"No," she answered immediately. "I didn't know that." Her voice was trembling a little.

Norm laughed shortly; he put the slug back in the box. "Go to sleep now," he murmured.

"Sorry, Norm?" Marge said. "I didn't hear you."

He looked up sharply at her. "I wasn't talking to you, Marge." He looked back at the box. "I wasn't talking to you at all."

Timmy Meade thought the fence frightened Sam Wentis and he wondered if he should ask him why. *Hey, Sam, why you scared of the shit damn fence*? But, he considered, you just didn't talk to Sam the way you talked to other kids.

"Look what it says here," Sam Wentis said. "It says 'Empire.' "

"That's the brand name, Sam."

" 'Empire'?"

"Yeah, 'cuz this is 'The Empire State.' Didn't you know that?"

Sam didn't answer.

Timmy repeated, "Didn't you know that, Sam—that this is . . ."

Sam turned his head suddenly, his eyes wide, his mouth tight. And Timmy Meade felt a quick, sharp chill take hold, as if, impossibly, his friend was somehow threatening him. He laughed a high, nervous, cackling laugh.

And a moment later, the laugh came back to him from somewhere in the woods just behind. And something about it—its pitch, its duration; he didn't know what, precisely—made him shudder.

He laughed again, louder and longer.

And he saw, as he laughed, that Sam Wentis was quickly scaling the six-foot-high Empire fence.

"Sam, what are you trying to do?" Because there were jagged spikes of fencing at the top. "Are you trying to hurt yourself? Shit damn, if you wanta hurt yourself, Sam, go ahead. I hope you slit your shit damn neck!"

Then he saw that Sam Wentis was straddling the top of the fence. In the next moment, he had jumped to the other side.

"Sam?" There was no response. Sam Wentis stood motionless on the opposite side of the fence.

On his eighth birthday, several years earlier, Timmy Meade received from his parents a big white rat. He named it Samson, for no particular reason, and kept it in a large wire cage. Six months later, he noticed that Samson had grown listless, that he had no appetite, that he'd even lost some weight. After a good deal of thought, Timmy decided that Samson wanted his freedom. The cage was large, yes, but a cage is, after all, just a cage, and no living thing was meant to spend its entire life in one. So, that afternoon, when Samson wasn't looking—because it was going to be a surprise—Timmy opened the cage door and left the room. When he came back a half hour later he saw two things: He saw that, somehow, the cage door had closed by itself, and he saw that Samson, having left the cage, was, grotesquely, trying to butt through the wire to return to it. A mass of dark blood covered his snout.

Watching Sam Wentis now, Timmy Meade saw that same awful, still panic, and fear and desperation he had seen then, and he said very soothingly, "Climb the fence again, Sam. Like you just did."

Sam Wentis said nothing.

"What you scared of, Sam?"

And when the next few moments had ended, when Sam Wentis was done trying to ram his body head first through the sturdy fence, when he lay quivering in a heap next to the fence, where it bulged most, Timmy Meade stared hard at him, whispered, "C'mon Sam, why'd you wanta go and do that?" Fifteen minutes later, he found himself back in Granada, pleading with Trudy Wentis (trimming rose bushes in her backyard), "It's Sam, please, it's Sam!" over and over again until, at last, she followed him.

*   *   *

The doctor shook his head incredulously. "From what his friend told me, Mr. and Mrs. Wentis, I'm surprised your son didn't do a lot more harm to himself."

Trudy Wentis said, "But . . . his face, Dr. Wilkins . . . it was covered with blood . . ."

"He opened a relatively large wound on his forehead, Mrs. Wentis; it took seven stitches to close it, and that's where the blood came from." He paused briefly, then continued, "He also sustained quite a few bruises and minor lacerations, but they're nothing to worry about. I *am* going to prescribe some painkillers, however. Those fingers"—Sam had broken three fingers on his right hand—"are going to give him a good deal of pain."

Dick Wentis asked tentatively, "Then we can take him home, Doctor?"

The doctor checked his watch. "Why don't we let him rest here for another hour or so, until four o'clock. We've got a nice little coffee shop down the hall." He nodded to the right. "You can grab a bite to eat, if you're hungry, and when you come back, I'll have that prescription and then you can take Sam home. Okay?"

Dick and Trudy both nodded; "Okay," Trudy said, and Dr. Wilkins hurried away.

Dick Wentis popped a cool, stiff french fry into his mouth. He grimaced. "Yuck!"

Trudy pushed her plate away. "I don't know why I ordered this," she murmured. "I'm not hungry."

"Nerves," Dick suggested. "You come to a restaurant and you're expected to order food. *They* expect it; *you* expect it. It's part of the rational order of things."

Trudy cut in, "Why in the hell would Sam do that? Why, Dick?"

"I don't understand him either, Trudy." He pushed his plate away. "Not all the time."

"I gave up trying to *understand* him a long time ago, Dick."

"Is that fair? To him, I mean."

"No. And I don't think I've given up, really. It's just that sometimes it takes so much effort . . ."

"I know." This was a conversation that was all too familiar to them both, and Dick thought that this time it was best to change the subject. "Tell me about Timmy Meade," he said. "Are he and Sam pretty close, do you think?"

Trudy smiled tentatively. "Sam and Timmy? Oh sure, but I don't think it'll last. I think they'll drift apart. Sam will find other friends, kids that are more his type . . ."

Dick harrumphed, "He sure won't find them in Granada."

Trudy looked questioningly at him.

"Haven't you noticed," he explained, "that Sam and Timmy are just about the only kids in the entire development? Maybe when other families move in—"

"But Dick, I heard them—in the woods."

"Heard who?"

"Children. I assumed they lived in Granada."

"No, there's just Sam and Timmy at the moment, as far as I know. Of course, as I said, when other families start moving in—"

"Maybe they were farm kids, Dick. Do you think they could have been farm kids?"

"In the woods? Sure, I guess so. I guess they'd have to be, wouldn't they?!"

"Yes, Dick, they would." She paused; she remembered the voices, and the laughter all around her as she tried, nearly in vain, to keep up with Timmy Meade. And she remembered thinking—hearing the voices of the children, and their laughter—*Why don't they help? Can't they see we're in trouble here?* Remembered calling out to them, futilely, "Can you help us, can you help us?" Remembered casting about for some glimpse of them and seeing only the random, changing patterns of late afternoon sunlight through the branches of evergreens and oaks and honey locusts. Remembered that at the fence, where they'd found Sam, the laughter and the crowd of voices had been loudest . . .

"Trudy, are you with us? Trudy?"

She came out of her reverie; she checked her watch. "Ten till four, Dick. Let's go."

"Okay," Dick said. He looked about, saw the waitress and motioned to her. "Check, please," he called.

Chapter 9

October 15

It was nice, Miles, Janice McIntyre wanted to say, to deny the truth, that it had been little more than a chore, something to do merely because it hadn't been done in so long. She reached across the bed and touched his cheek tentatively; she said nothing.

"Could you turn the light on, Janice?" he said.

She stood, switched the overhead light on; she squinted at the sudden brightness.

"I'm sorry, Janice." He thought a moment. "About the lovemaking."

"Why, Miles? I'm not."

"I know you're not." It was an offhanded remark; he wasn't sure where to go with it. He swung his feet to the floor and sat up.

"Sometimes, Miles," Janice said, "it's great. Sometimes it's good." She got her oversized red velour robe out of the closet and shrugged into it. "This time, it was good."

He looked questioningly at her. "You going somewhere?"

She nodded. "Downstairs. I'm hungry."

He glanced at the alarm clock. "At this hour?"

"It's a craving, Miles. You've heard of cravings. They happen to pregnant women." She put her slippers on, went to the bedroom door, opened it. "Do you want anything?"

"No. Thanks." He lay back suddenly, threw his arms straight up over his head. "I'm beat."

"You're getting old, Miles," she said, and she left the room.

He listened—exhaustion rapidly catching up with him—to her soft footfalls on the hardwood floor as she made her way to the top of the stairs. "Turn the light on, Janice," he called.

"I'm okay," she called back, at once annoyed and at the same time comforted by his protectiveness. But he was halfway into sleep already and hadn't heard her.

The little breakfast nook, she thought, was becoming her own private place to be alone, to think.

It had been a smooth and quick transition, she decided, from her good feelings at the apartment (feelings she had nurtured for almost seven years) to her good feelings here, in this house, big as it was, and new (and therefore strange) as it was, and quiet as it was. She thought the quiet had a lot to do with it, and she was sure that in time, when the dozen or so other families moved into Granada, it would change. But, for now, she had the quiet. And the darkness. And the good feelings.

She let her gaze wander idly over the softly

spotlit backyard; she imagined winter resting heavily on the small tool shed, and on the white marble birdbath, and the four flowering dogwood trees. She liked winter. She imagined that winter in Granada would be something very special.

She accepted the gentle touch of a hand on her shoulder as Miles's hand. She said, "You should be asleep." The idea that he'd come downstairs bothered her; he couldn't help but see that in the last few weeks these "private moments" had become very precious to her. She smiled to cover her annoyance, and reached behind and to her left for the light switch. She thought about their lovemaking earlier that evening; it was probably what he wanted to talk about. She switched the light on and turned quickly in the seat.

She noted first the heavy odor of something burning and wondered fleetingly why one of the ceiling-mounted smoke alarms hadn't gone off. She thought it was woodsmoke she smelled; woodsmoke and, underneath it, barely noticeable, the acrid smell of burning hair. She grimaced. "Miles!" she called, not nearly loud enough, because, she knew, if the house was on fire she didn't want to know about it. Not yet, anyway.

"Miles!" she called again, but no louder. She tried to stand, and couldn't. Because the gentle touch at her shoulder had strengthened enormously. "Please," she whispered. "Please," she repeated.

And then she heard the loud, insane, staccato crackling of the fire all around and she whispered "Please" again; then she shouted it, her head darting from right to left in a futile search for the flames.

The quiet settled over her again like a quick sleep.

The smell of woodsmoke and burning hair ended in the same moment.

She murmured her husband's name once more. And fainted.

Chapter 10

Shelly and Malcolm Harris

Lorraine Graham and her twin sons Robert and Robin

The fifth and sixth families to move into Granada were Shelly and Malcolm Harris, proud parents of a seven-month-old baby daughter named Serena, and Lorraine Graham, widowed mother of twin thirteen-year-old boys named Robin and Robert. They all came to Granada on the same day—a bright, warm Sunday late in October. Shelly Harris said to Lorraine Graham, when her family's moving-in process was half done, "It's the only place to bring a child up. I'm convinced of that," and she gestured expansively to indicate Granada and what was, as far as she was concerned, the wilderness surrounding it. Lorraine Graham agreed completely. "It's a move that Stan and I had been planning for a long, long time." She broke down momentarily, remembering her late husband—Shelly pretended not to notice—and concluded, "I think the boys and I will be very happy here. I grew up on a farm, you know, and this"—she gestured in much the way that Shelly had—"is almost nostalgic. All that's missing is the smell of cow manure and wet hay, and those are things I'll gladly do without."

Shelly nodded. "Malcolm—that's my husband—suffers from hay fever. Our daughter, Serena—she's with her grandmother today—has no allergies at all, thank God."

The two women continued chatting for nearly an hour. They agreed several times that Granada would someday be quite beautiful—"Once those ugly bulldozers are taken away," Lorraine said. "And once they finish laying all that pipe. What is that? Is that sewer pipe?" Shelly said she wasn't sure, that she'd have to ask her husband.

And they introduced themselves to two of their neighbors—Marge Gellis and Dora Meade, who stopped briefly, within minutes of each other, to talk. Shelly and Lorraine agreed that Marge was, as Shelly put it, "a little dowdy, but nice enough," and that Dora, according to Lorraine, "will probably take some getting used to. She seems a little hard around the edges."

Lorraine and her sons, Robin and Robert (who, Malcolm Harris commented later, seemed to giggle more than two young boys ought to) had dinner that night at the Harris home. Lorraine felt, thankfully, that she had a great, new friend in Shelly Harris.

Around Granada, autumn was settling in. It was slow in coming this year; the summer had lingered lazily, well into October. Even the nights stayed warm. Then, toward the end of the month, the air grew chill and for the very first time, a still, ragged, horizontal line of chimney smoke, caught in a freak temperature inversion, hung over the small cluster of inhabited houses.

Outside Granada, in the stand of woods a half mile to the west, in the fields of quack grass, in the long-untended apple orchards to the north, the sudden rush of autumn caught many creatures by surprise. A gaggle of Canadian geese, which had early in the afternoon stopped to water itself at a small, stagnant pond, hurried noisily into the air again; it would soon stop somewhere else. Only the first snowstorm would push the geese on in earnest.

A hundred thousand grasshoppers and a million crickets finished their lives quickly, leaving their egg sacs behind for the spring:

And in several places, the autumn came and brought fear with it. It was the fear caused by ignorance, and pain, and knowledge—the knowledge that in the winter's cold, death came. It was the way of things.

And the eyes that studied Granada, that studied the pretty line of chimney smoke, and the warm lights, and the dark shapes of the houses, saw all of it now with the very crude beginnings of understanding.

Laughter, like small, dense flights of insects, rose up in several places that night and dissipated very slowly in the still air.

Norm Gellis owned two long-guns—a thirty-five-year-old Remington 760 pump-action rifle, and a Weatherby 20-gauge, semi-automatic over-and-under shotgun. Both guns were kept standing, barrel up, in a locked closet in his bedroom. Twice a year, on his birthday (because the rifle had been an eighteenth-birthday gift from his father) and on Christmas Eve (because Marge had given him the shotgun fifteen years earlier as a Christmas gift; "I'm going to take up hunting again, Marge," he'd told her), he cleaned the guns thoroughly. The cleanings were essentially unnecessary because he had never used the shotgun, and had fired the rifle only five times, on various hunting trips with his father. Beyond wounding a doe very slightly on one of those trips, he had never hit anything. He was a terrible shot; "You're too nervous," his father told him. "Why are you so damned nervous?" But the young Norm could only grin stupidly and plead ignorance. He didn't want to explain that, drawn as he was to "the overwhelming thrill of the hunt" (as his father put it), long-guns frightened him overwhelmingly. He thought that if there were such a thing as "instant shellshock" then he had it, and it was incurable. It was the noise, he felt certain, and the vibration, and the recoil. And perhaps there were some other factors—the weight and size of the gun, for instance—but he had never taken the time to think it through completely. His father had called him a coward on their final hunting trip, and he didn't want to find, upon self-examination, that it was true.

He thought the Smith & Wesson Model 12 .38 Police Special he held on his open right hand now was quite a striking little piece of equipment. Small, blunt-nosed, easily concealed. He had fired it several dozen times, and it was loud, sure, but not nearly as loud as the damned long-guns, and the recoil was practically nonexistent. And he had found that, remarkably, his confidence with the gun had made him into a passable marksman. (He had been taught the bent-legged, straight-armed, two-handed method of firing; he thought it looked good on him.)

Marge, across the living room from him, looked up from her magazine. "Norm, I'm really very uncomfortable with that thing around." She had been toying with the proper words for half an hour, ever since Norm had gotten the gun from its hiding place ("You'd put a big hole in yourself, Marge, so to keep you from messin' with it, I'm gonna hide it. Okay?"), but, after the words came out, she thought she might have offended him, so she immediately attempted to amend the words: "I don't mean . . . please don't think I'm afraid of it."

He cut in, grinning, "Hey, listen, I know this weapon makes you 'uncomfortable,' and I wish I could help that, Marge, I really do. But you wanta know what makes *me* uncomfortable? I'll tell you what makes *me* uncomfortable, Marge. It makes me uncomfortable to think that while we're asleep up there"—he pointed with the gun to indicate their bedroom—"asleep and *vul*nerable, some lousy *trespasser* can just waltz in here and do whatever he wants. In *our* house!" His grin became a tight, malicious leer. "And you know what the law says I can *do* with that trespasser, Marge? That trespasser in *my* house! The law says I can't do a goddamned thing. The law says if I blow him away, if I hurt one little hair on his precious little head, Marge, then *I'm* the one who gets thrown in the cage, like *I'm* the one who's the goddamned animal. And that's why I got this goddamned gun, Marge. 'Cuz the fuckin' law is fuckin' wrong, 'cuz the next time *this* house gets broken into–"

"But, Norm, he was just a boy–"

He held his hand up to quiet her. She stopped talking abruptly. "I'm going to tell you something, Marge, something from when I was in 'Nam, something I've never told you—"

" 'Nam?"

"Vi*et* Nam. We fought a losin' war there, Marge. Remember?"

Marge nodded, embarrassed. "You never told me you were in Viet Nam." She tried to smile, as if suddenly proud of him.

"Yes, I was, Marge." It was a lie. "Saw three years of combat, and I want to tell you a story from those years, and if you'll stop interrupting me, I'll tell it." He paused; she said nothing; it was his cue. "Okay. We were in Khe San, just outside Saigon—that was the capital of 'Nam, you remember that, Marge? And it was the closin' days of the war, the last few days, and we were all itchin' to get outa there 'cuz we knew the communists was on their way. And there I was with my buddy, Frank Thompson—I ever tell you about him?—and we were patrolling this street, you know, for snipers, and I was talkin' to Frank about one thing and another, and, all of a sudden, Frank grabs his chest, and falls straight to his knees. 'Norm?' he says, and then he falls flat on his face. Dead!" He paused for effect.

Marge said, "He had a heart attack, Norm?"

Norm rolled his eyes. "Jesus, Marge. What do you mean heart attack!! In 'Nam, for Christ's sake?! He got shot right through the heart, just like 50,000 other guys, only he didn't get it from no Viet Cong, at least not from a grownup one. I *know* that, Marge, 'cuz when I look up, I see this kid, about 50 yards away, and he's maybe nine or ten—the same age as that kid who broke in here—and this kid has this sickening grin on his face, and this government issue rifle in his hands, and he says something like 'I got him, I got him!' And then he runs off."

Norm paused again for effect. Marge said nothing; she looked ill at ease.

"That's a true story, Marge, true as yesterday." He nodded at the Smith & Wesson still in his hand. "And it's one reason I got this little beauty, and one reason I'm going to use it, if I got to—if I'm forced to use it."

Marge's hands began to tremble. The magazine she had been pretending to read fell to the floor. "That's an awful story, Norm." She bent forward and picked up the magazine; a ludicrous, quivering smile appeared on her lips. "That's an awful story, Norm." She stood abruptly and put the magazine on a small table near her chair. "I'm going to go to bed now. I'm tired, Norm." She continued smiling; she made her way to the living room doorway; she paused. "Are you coming up, Norm?"

"This weapon needs cleaning, Marge. I practiced with it today, so now I got to clean it. Guns are just like pets, Marge. You got to tend to 'em all the time."

"Yes," she said, in a monotone. "I understand that." And she left the room.

Norm listened as she padded up the stairs. Her steps were slow and deliberate. She sounded very old and very tired.

*　　　*　　　*

By midnight, the still, ragged line of chimney smoke was gone, pushed off by a sudden strong wind. Several poorly installed roofing tiles on one of Granada's not-yet-completed houses were whisked away by the wind. The smallest of the four flowering dogwood trees in the McIntyres' backyard was partially uprooted. At the Harris home, some empty garbage cans, still awaiting the white aluminum sheds that sheltered all garbage cans in Granada, rolled noisily across the side yard and into the Harrises' new Mercury Bobcat.

From their bedroom window on the second floor of the Graham house next door, Robin and Robert Graham fell into fits of nervous giggling. Rolling garbage cans were hilarious things, as far as they were concerned. At the end of one giggling fit, Robert (Rob) Graham said to his brother, "It's a good thing they weren't fulla banana peels and melon rinds," which set them both up for another fit of giggling.

"Yeah," Robin managed.

"Banana peels and melon rinds," Rob said again, suddenly aware that the words felt good rolling off his tongue. "Ba-na-na peels," he sang, to no particular melody, "and melon rinds." Then he felt his brother elbow him hard in the ribs. "Hey, that hurts!"

Robin pointed urgently at the front of the Harrises' yard; "Looka that!"

Rob looked. He saw only the line of shrubs that the landscapers had put in the week before. Granada's three streets boasted a half-dozen street lamps—the far half of the line of shrubs was bathed now in the light from one of them.

"I don't see nothin'," Rob said, and he made a show of massaging his ribs.

"Well, they hid or somethin'," Robin said. "They hid behind the shrubberies." He looked questioningly at his brother; another giggle burst from him, but it was short-lived and anxious. "Some kids, Rob. Three of 'em. And one was a girl, and they didn't have no *clothes* on!" He paused to relish what he was saying. "They didn't have no clothes on," he repeated wonderingly, as if in fascination. "And they were just standin' there—the three of 'em—just standin' there looking up at me." He turned quickly, ran to the tall walnut bookshelf he and his brother shared, got a pair of binoculars off one of the shelves.

And the door burst open.

Lorraine Graham, still wrapping a short, white terrycloth robe around herself, moved quickly to the window and drew the curtains closed. "What in the *hell* are you boys doing?"

Rob, the twin still at the window, began to explain, "Robin said–"

And Robin interrupted hurriedly, "We weren't doin' nothin', Mom. We were watchin' trash cans blow around, that's all." He put the binoculars away, confident she hadn't seen them. "Just watchin' trash cans blow around," he repeated.

Lorraine Graham looked suspiciously at him: "Uh-huh," she said and nodded briskly to indicate their beds. "I'll give you five seconds!" she ordered. They obeyed instantly, and moments later she left the room.

"I don't know," Robin said breathlessly from his bed, as if in answer to a question his brother hadn't asked. "I guess she was thirteen or fourteen. And you know"—he grinned and made cupping motions in the dark with his hands at his chest—"she had these great little boobs, like Mom has," which made his brother very uncomfortable because he wasn't sure he liked the idea that his mother had breasts at all, let alone that Robin would talk about them. "You'll see," Robin went on, still grinning, still awed by what he'd seen.

Outside, Granada was quiet. The wind had died as quickly as it had come up.

And those that watched were sleeping. In their way.

Part Four

NIGHT FIRES

Chapter 11

November 1 ·

Manny Kent hit the brake pedal; the old Chevy pulled hard to the right and came to a halt on the soft shoulder, its back end out in the middle of the narrow dirt road.

"Friggin' brakes!" Manny hissed. "It was just like the friggin' battery, all the time leakin' acid, and the friggin' gas lines! Damned friggin' old hunka junk!"

He turned, got Clyde's 30.30 from the back seat, a box of cartridges from the glove compartment. Then, because the Chevy's driver's door wouldn't open—the lock had broken closed several years before—he slid across the seat, opened the passenger door, and climbed out, cartridges in one hand, rifle in the other.

He shivered, set the rifle against the car, buttoned the top button of his denim jacket. "Je-*sus*!" he murmured. He blamed Sarah, his wife, for the fact that he was out here on this godawful, cold November day: It was her damned nagging, wasn't it, that had driven him from the house an hour before (because, he knew, if he'd stayed and tried to listen to her he'd sure as hell do something stupid, like let her have it—*whammo!*—right in the chops. And nothing good would come of that, only a couple days in John Hastings's lousy jail).

He picked the rifle up and looked about. He thought briefly of getting back in the Chevy and letting his anger cool at The Playground (Penn Yann's only combination bar and pizza parlor), then decided, no, what he really wanted to do was some serious thinking. About himself. And Sarah. And their marriage. And whether it was worth all the grief it gave him. He knew it wasn't, that what he'd really come out here to think about, while his anger cooled, was the best way of telling Sarah that their marriage was on the shit pile.

He tucked the butt of the rifle under his right arm—barrel pointing at the ground—and walked off the road, into the stunted grass and weeds, toward the Empire fence a hundred yards away. He realized at once that his anger had cooled tremendously in the last few minutes. He didn't know why exactly. Maybe it had something to do with being alone, with the gun, and the idea that, with a little luck—which was way overdue—he'd get that deer he'd missed a month ago, the day he and Clyde found what was left of the colored man. (He put the next thought out of his head immediately. He feared Clyde, and Clyde had warned him again and again about even mentioning the colored man's pure silver bracelet to anyone, let alone picking it up and trying to get a mortgage payment paid with it.) And so, when he passed within a couple of feet of the spot, he turned his head slightly, saw the "white rock" and quickened his pace.

And soon found that he was running. Away from the white rock. And the pure silver bracelet tucked beneath it. And the murder that had been done there. And the ghost of the colored man, which had surely fallen into stride just behind him, and was surely grinning, and stretching out its long arms, reaching madly for him . . .

As if in a panic, Manny tossed the gun over the Empire fence, failed to note where it had fallen, scaled the fence in seconds, jumped to the other side. And stood panting breathlessly, eyes on the white rock, fifty yards away, and on the fence that separated him from the thing—the ghost of the colored man—that guarded it.

After a moment, Manny cursed. Jesus, it was okay to scare yourself. Lots of fun. But to go and throw your brother-in-law's 30.30 into the damned bushes as a result, and maybe to lose it—that was just plain dumb. He cursed again. He looked to his right, his left, tried to put himself mentally back in the same spot and in the same stance he'd been in moments before, when he'd tossed the rifle over the fence. Once more, he cursed. Because his memory failed him. Because the thickets were too dense—incredibly dense. And he pictured himself crawling around on his hands and knees for a week of Sundays looking for the goddamned rifle.

He saw it then, just an arm's length away, barrel up, half-concealed in the thickets. He sighed, withdrew it from the thickets. And decided that the

damned buck he'd seen a month ago was going to
be his. He deserved it!

He put the butt of the rifle under his arm; he
walked quickly along the fence. Within minutes,
he came upon a clearing in the thickets. "Yes, sir!"
he muttered. "Yes sir!" he said aloud, and he stepped
into the clearing.

He stopped immediately so his eyes could adjust
to the sudden dim light here, at the perimeter of
the small stand of woods. He thought he was probably trespassing, that if he bothered to look he'd
see a dozen posted signs to that effect. But heck,
who was to know? And while he thought of this he
watched, only a little puzzled, as the trunk of an
oak nearby moved rhythmically, in and out, as if it
were breathing, and he decided that a person's
eyes played tricks on him when they were coming
in from the light to the darkness. Like he just had.
Then he saw that what he'd thought was part of
the tree trunk was really a smooth, naked, dark
back, and long, dark hair, and the side of a wonderfully rounded buttock.

He froze. Something inside him—some little-used,
self-protective sixth sense—froze him. And it told
him that something wasn't quite right here, that
the child he was seeing—the young girl, he realized now, as she turned to face him—wasn't playing
hooky from school, and wasn't the child of some
neighbor back in town, and didn't belong to someone in that new housing development just a couple stones' throws away. He thought, fleetingly,
that it was her huge, pale blue eyes that told him
all this, and the blank, expressionless line of her
mouth, and her naked, exquisite, and impossible
beauty . . .

"Yes, sir!" she said. "Yes sir!" she repeated.

Manny Kent's mouth dropped open. He decided, on the instant, that only the devil himself could push his—Manny Kent's—whining scratchy voice up through that young girl's throat.

"Yes, sir!" she said again.

Manny brought the 30.30 up very slowly, mechanically, to a firing position. He aimed, his focus on the sight, not on his target, just as he'd been taught. And he realized that he hadn't loaded the rifle. He froze again.

The child had vanished.

Manny screamed—a high-pitched, shrill, animal-like scream that was repeated immediately, all around him.

Something touched him softly, here and there—on his legs, his buttocks, his groin, as if caterpillars were launching themselves at him from the leaves overhead.

Fifteen Years Earlier

Paul Griffin moved south, off the path and into his fields.

He stopped again. He watched quietly, reverently. He owed them that much. His curses, his anger had no place here, in their midst. This was their cathedral.

And as he watched, and saw their faces turn occasionally, saw their eyes, expressionless, look in his direction, watched the firelight play on their smooth, dark skin, watched hands touch hands, and arms, and bellies—as if giving warmth and receiving it, as if re-experiencing and reveling in what they were—he knew that they were doing him a kindness, that he was privileged somehow. That few men, if any, had been allowed to see what he was seeing.

Manny let go of the rifle. It dropped dully to the ground at his feet.

"Ba-na-na peels and mel-on rinds," he heard, and the Manny Kent deep inside him—the Manny Kent climbing out of the Chevy, running from the ghost of the colored man, scaling the Empire fence—laughed hysterically.

The small, soft hands at his throat cut the laughter off abruptly. He slumped to his knees.

"Ba-na-na peels and mel-on rinds," he heard again. "Yes, sir!"

Janice McIntyre lowered herself very slowly into the seat at the breakfast nook. *Two* weeks, she thought, because that was how long it had taken her to force herself back here. Two weeks, and now this little private place to be alone, to think, was hers again. She had begun to exorcise the ghost.

She grinned self-critically. "Prepartum hallucinations," Miles had suggested, and she remembered laughing at him; "That's a new one on me, Miles." He'd shrugged; "Well, you never know, Janice." And that was true enough.

She glanced over at the clock on the stove: 4:45. Miles would be home in a half hour, and he'd expect something in the way of a supper—a TV dinner, some quick tuna casserole. She sighed. Miles was going to have to wait, because staying put here, at this damned haunted breakfast nook, had top priority this afternoon.

She sniffed the air tentatively, then quite conspicuously. She sighed again. Only the odor of Spic and Span, and a country autumn, and, beneath it all, the odor of her own nervous sweat. No woodsmoke. No burning hair (she grimaced).

"Have you hit your head recently?" the doctor had asked.

"No," she'd answered.

"Because unusual odors, without a physical cause, are one of the symptoms of concussion," he'd told her.

She thought now that she didn't *remember* hitting her head, anyway, at least not hard enough to cause a concussion. But then, that was often difficult to pin down, too, because—the doctor went on—even an apparently slight blow on the wrong part of the head can cause a lot of damage.

She realized that she was grasping at straws. Prepartum hallucinations, concussion, hunger pangs, for Christ's sake! She had experienced what she had experienced and she was keeping herself seated here, at the breakfast nook, because she had to overcome it, because she had to put it behind her once and for all, because if she didn't—

Her peripheral vision told her that the woman was standing motionless in the kitchen doorway:

"No," Janice whispered. "No! Please! Go away!" She closed her eyes tightly. "Please go away, please, please go away!"

"Janice?"

Janice's breathing halted momentarily. She turned her head. Trudy Wentis smiled quizzically at her.

"Janice, I'm sorry, but I've been ringing your door-bell for the past fifteen minutes. I thought something might be wrong, so I came in. Your door was unlocked. Are you all right?"

"Oh my God, Trudy, you have no idea—"

Trudy Wentis crossed the room quickly and sat across from Janice at the breakfast nook. She felt sure she was intruding, and equally sure that Janice needed to talk to someone. (Theirs was a friend-ship which had been kindled a week earlier, when Miles left for a two-day business trip and asked Trudy if she could "sort of keep an eye on my wife, if you don't mind." And then he'd added that Janice was "pregnant and nervous. She doesn't like to be alone.")

"Janice, would you like to talk about it?" Trudy said now.

"There's nothing to talk about."

"Okay." Soothingly.

"Unless you want to talk about ghosts. Do you want to talk about ghosts, Trudy?"

"Any ghost in particular?"

A slight, sad smile appeared on Janice's face. "My own, if I keep this up—high blood pressure, ulcers . . ."

In the still, cold November air, a scream settled over Granada from the small stand of woods a half mile off. Timmy Meade, just getting off his school-bus, heard it—*A hawk*, he decided, because he felt sure that "country living" was turning him into a junior naturalist.

Lorraine Graham, making her sons' beds, win-dows open to the country air, heard it and dismissed it immediately because it could only be what it appeared to be—the scream of someone in deep torment—and that, of course, was impossible here, in Granada.

At the McIntyre house, the two women seated at the breakfast nook, absorbed in their conversation, heard nothing at all.

Chapter 12

Norm Gellis couldn't sleep. It was, he felt sure, because of all the coffee Marge had pushed at him after dinner—"Oh, have some more, Norm; stay and talk with us. Mother doesn't visit that often, you know." He had very grudgingly assented, and now he thought he was paying the price.

He listened to Marge snoring softly in her bed. "Damn you!" he whispered, and was on the verge of damning her mother, too (she had left shortly after supper), when a slight, barely audible tinkling noise drifted up to him from somewhere on the first floor. He pushed himself up on his elbows: "Marge?" he whispered anxiously. "I think somebody's in the house, Marge." There was a hint of excitement in his voice. "Wake up, Marge!" he said aloud. He listened; Marge continued snoring. "Bitch!"

He sat up, paused, heard the tinkling noise again;

117

he smiled. "I'm going downstairs, Marge." She continued snoring. "I'm going to get the .38 and go downstairs." The tempo and pitch of her snoring altered. "It's okay, Marge—go back to sleep." He stood and moved quickly and quietly into the bathroom, the smile stuck on his face all the while. He opened a cupboard beneath the sink, got down on one knee, felt inside the cupboard on a small ledge inside a narrow panel above the cupboard door. He heard the quick, brittle noise of glass breaking somewhere on the first floor. "Shit!" he murmured, still smiling. He got the .38 from its hiding place, went back to the bedroom. Miraculously, Marge was still asleep. He went to the top of the stairs, wondered if he should turn on the overhead light in the living room with the switch up here, in the hallway. He quickly decided, no, the element of surprise was very important now.

Putting his weight on the extreme right-hand side of the steps, close to the wall—where the wood was least likely to creak—he started down. "Shit!" he whispered, spontaneously, gleefully.

The ringing of the telephone woke Clyde Watkins almost immediately. In the two decades that he'd served as Penn Yann's Volunteer Fire Chief he had taught himself to sleep, as he put it, "with one ear and one eye open." He snatched the receiver up. "Yes?"

"Clyde, it's me, Sarah."

He rolled his eyes. "Christ, Sarah, have you got any idea what time it is?"

"Three thirty, Clyde. That's why I called." She hesitated. "Manny's been gone since yesterday afternoon, Clyde, and I'm worried about him."

"He's probably sleepin' off a drunk somewhere, Sarah."

"I don't think so, Clyde. I called The Playground and Itzy's and Bagnano's, too. He ain't been in none of 'em all night. Nobody's seen him, Clyde."

"We got a liquor store in town, Sarah—"

"I called there too, Clyde. And like I said, no one's seen him. And I'm real worried, Clyde. I was hopin' you'd have some idea where he might be. I thought he might be with you, as a matter of fact."

Clyde sat up reluctantly. He shivered: Damn, it was cold! "He ain't with me, Sarah."

"Can you go lookin' for him, Clyde?" she pleaded. "Can you do that for me?"

"I was just about to, Sarah."

"Thank you, Clyde. I knew you'd help."

"Don't I always, Sarah?"

"You want me to come with you, Clyde? Where you think yer gonna look? You'd tell me if he's got a girlfriend, wouldn'tcha, Clyde? You'd tell me that . . ."

"He ain't got no girlfriend, Sarah. Who in hell'd want him?!"

"That ain't nice, Clyde." But she knew the question was a good one. "I'm puttin' my coat on right this minute, Clyde. I'll be waitin' for ya."

"Okay, Sarah." He sighed. "I'll be over directly." He hung up, shivered again. *Unseasonably cold, tonight,* he remembered the TV weatherman saying. *Into the teens in some of the valley areas . . . By early morning the temperature should be on the rise again.* He stood and put his jeans and flannel shirt on over thermal underwear. It was early morning, now, wasn't it?! he asked himself. And still it was colder than a witch's tit!

He got his heavy winter coat out of the closet and put it on. He had no idea where he'd look first for his brother-in-law. If Manny hadn't been in any of the bars, and he wasn't at home, well then, where else could he be? He was a real predictable son of a bitch, Clyde thought, and that fact told him that something was very, very wrong.

Lorraine Graham pushed her twins' bedroom door open quickly, so as to catch them by surprise. "You boys had better—" she began, and fell silent. Robin and Robert Graham were sleeping quietly in their separate beds. Lorraine's brow furrowed; she closed their door gently. She felt certain she'd heard them talking and giggling (Christ, but why did they *giggle*, for God's sake?). She pulled her short, terrycloth robe tight around her. The next time she went into Penn Yann, she decided, she'd have to check the prices on good, winter-type robes. This thing she was wearing was obviously meant more for seduction than warmth. She started for her bedroom, her steps made uneven and uncertain by the interruption of sleep.

She heard the sound of her boys giggling again.

She hurried back to their room, threw the door open.

Robin lifted his head a little from the pillow. "Mom? What's the matter?"

She stared incredulously at him. "What do you mean, 'What's the matter?' You know damned well what the matter is."

Robin pulled his blanket up around his neck. "No, I don't, Mom," he stammered. "Could I have another blanket, Mom?"

Robert woke. "What's goin' on? Is it time for school?" He started to get out of bed, Lorraine shook her head; "No, Robert—you've got a couple hours' sleep left." She paused—her sudden anger had quickly given way to confusion. "You boys have been asleep all this time?"

"Yes, Mom," Robin answered.

Robert said nothing. He was asleep again.

"Oh," Lorraine said. And she left the room.

The smell of Norm Gellis's nervous perspiration roughly approximated the smell of vegetable soup. It was a smell that permeated the air around him now, and made his nose wrinkle. He had his finger on the downstairs light switch and was toying with several ideas. The first told him it was probably best to give his trespasser fair warning—something like, *Freeze, or you're a dead man!* Or maybe, *I got a .38 here, and I hate to tell ya what size hole it'll put in your belly!* Because, said the small voice of his intellect, the abrupt turning on of the light might panic the trespasser, and if the trespasser had a gun, too ... Which was why he much preferred the second idea. Surprise. Sudden and sure! And anyway, said the same, small voice, why give the trespasser fair warning?

He flicked the light on, took his military stance—bent-legged, straight-armed, a two-handed grip on the .38.

And he heard frantic, scrambling, scratching sounds on the hardwood floor to his right, near the entrance to the kitchen. He moved forward a few feet, the sweat suddenly pouring out of him, his legs still bent. He stopped and saw a flurry of

movement in the darkened kitchen. "Okay there,"
he yelled, his voice cracking slightly, "you freeze!"
And he fired the .38. It discharged dully and, at
the same moment, he heard Marge scream from
above. "Shit!" he murmured. "Go back to sleep,
Marge!" he called over his shoulder, suddenly
irritated.

He moved awkwardly into the kitchen, his legs
still bent, the gun still in its straight-armed, two-
handed grip. He heard a low, humorless chuckle
from deep within his chest.

And then he heard Marge scream again, closer,
on the upstairs landing, and he turned his head
slightly. "Marge"—still irritated beneath his chuckling—"it's *okay*, Marge!" He switched the kitchen
light on, crouched even lower. He quickly scanned
the room.

And sensed Marge behind him, in the kitchen
doorway. He continued scanning the room, chuckling all the while.

Marge screamed a third time. Loud.

He whirled, took one hand from the .38, and
slapped her hard. She stumbled backward, tried to
steady herself, and fell to the floor; a fourth, off-
pitch scream erupted from her.

Norm Gellis hissed, "Marge, will you *shut* up!
Can't you see I'm trying to *do* something here?!"

She stopped screaming abruptly. Her eyes widened, her lower lip trembled.

"And cover yourself, Marge." She wore white
cotton panties and a pink flannel, long-sleeved
pajama top. "There's *some*body in the house!"

He turned and scanned the kitchen again. He
saw the open door to the cellar. "Marge, did you

leave the cellar door open?" He waited, got no
response. "Marge, I asked you a question." Still
nothing. "Damn!" he whispered. He moved slowly
toward the door, the .38 once again in its two-
handed, straight-armed grip:

The irregular splotches of blood on the blue linoleum started him chuckling again—louder, in his
throat. "I got him, Marge!" he said. "I got the
bastard!"

Chapter 13

Clyde Watkins leaned across the seat and opened the pickup truck's passenger door. "Hi, Sarah."

Sarah climbed in and fastened her seat belt hurriedly. ("I feel naked without it," she had explained more than once.) She turned her head, attempted a smile. "Hi, Clyde. Thanks for stoppin'. I woke you up, didn't I?"

"It ain't the first time, Sarah." He put the truck in gear.

"Where we goin', Clyde?"

"Yer husband took my thirty-ought-thirty, Sarah, so I got a fair idea where he is." He punched the accelerator; the pickup lurched away from Sarah's mobile home:

"Why didn'tcha tell me about the rifle before, Clyde?" she said.

"He didn't borrow it, Sarah, he *took* it. Right outa this truck." He inclined his head toward the empty gun rack behind them. "I didn't find out till I come to get you."

Sarah looked confusedly at him: "You mean he's *huntin'*, Clyde? Then why's he been gone so long?"

Clyde chose not to answer. He knew that Sarah would realize the answers to her questions soon enough. She did. "Oh my God!" she whispered.

Clyde reached across the seat and patted her hand. "Now, Sarah, don't go imaginin' things, it won't do no one no good."

"Clyde, he's *shot* himself, I know it. That damn fool's shot himself, just like your Uncle Winston—"

Clyde braked hard for a flashing red light; he looked left and right, saw no headlights; he hit the accelerator. "We don't *know* he's shot himself, Sarah, and until we do—" He stopped in midsentence. Sarah had begun to weep.

"We're gonna find him all shot up, ain't we, Clyde? With a great big hole in his chest or in his head, ain't that right, Clyde?"

He turned the pickup sharply left. "You calm down right now, Sarah, or I'm lettin' you out."

She continued to weep. She made no reply.

Lorraine Graham thought, *I'm losing control of those boys. They need Stan—he's firmer than I.* And she rolled quickly in the bed, from her back to her side, as if that physical movement would put her mind on something else, something that didn't turn around and bite its own tail, as her thoughts of her dead husband invariably did.

She let her eyes open. "Bastard!" she said. "Bastard!" to leave her with two young boys who giggled too much, and with the awful job of finding someone new for them, and for herself (and in the meantime to be what she could never be—both mother and father to the boys).

And "Bastard!" because she spent her nights so very much alone and so very much in *need* . . .

She focused on the closed bedroom door, only a vague, whitish outline in the dark, and she imagined Stan pushing it open, imagined him crossing the room to her. Touching her. Holding her.

"Bastard!" she said again, because he'd extracted that damned promise from her that this house would be where Robin and Robert "turned into men." "Bastard!" for that idealism and that chauvinism, because this house was really no different, was it, than a city apartment? There were still the (displaced) city people, only far fewer of them (and she wanted to be alone, yes, yes, but not that alone). . . . Christ! If only the lousy bastard were here with her now!

Sarah asked, "Where you takin' us, Clyde? Is this where you and Manny used to hunt?"

"Uh-huh," Clyde answered. "Up the road a bit." He nodded.

Because of a heavy overcast, the darkness beyond the pickup truck and its headlights was nearly total. Sarah held her watch up so she could read it by the light from the dashboard: 3:55. "Shit, Clyde— what we gonna do out there, now? We gotta wait till the sun comes up."

"I got a couple flashlights." He reached, opened the glove compartment; there was a large silver-colored flashlight in it. "There's one," he said. "And I got another one in a tool chest back there." He indicated the bed of the pickup, then closed the glove compartment.

"I can't do that, Clyde."

He looked questioningly at her. "Can't do what?"

"I can't go prowlin' around out there in the pitch dark."

"You wanta wait in the truck?"

"Yes, Clyde—'less you got some objections."

"I got no objections, Sarah. Maybe yer husband will, but I don't." He turned his head briefly and grinned at her.

He saw her straight-arm the dashboard suddenly: "Clyde, look out!"

He turned back. "Oh Jesus!" And hit the brake hard, pulled the wheel to the left. He heard the grating, shrill screech of metal against metal as the pickup connected with the back end of Manny's Chevy. A half second later, the pickup shuddered to a halt. "Christ almighty!" Clyde muttered. His hands were shaking; he gripped the steering wheel hard; he looked at Sarah; "You okay?" She was rubbing the side of her head, had obviously hit it against the passenger window. "Yeah, I guess." She winced, turned to look at the car they'd hit. "That's our Biscayne, Clyde—that damned fool husbanda mine parked it right in the middle of the road! What'd he do that for, Clyde?" She was on the verge of hysteria. "What in hell would he go and do that for, Clyde, why would he—"

Clyde slapped her; her hysteria ended abruptly. He looked her squarely in the eye. "I'm gonna go check the damage to the truck, Sarah. You understand me? I'm gonna go check the damage, and I want you to wait right here."

She nodded once, quickly, her eyes wide. "I'm sorry, Clyde."

"No need." He got the flashlight from the glove

compartment and climbed out of the truck. "Stay put, for now," he called. He aimed the flashlight at the truck's left rear tire. He groaned. "Christ almighty!" He shone the flashlight on Sarah; she put her hand up against the glare. "Clyde!" she protested. He turned the light off. "Whole damned wheel's about six inches back of where it should be, Sarah, and the tire's flat besides." He turned the flashlight on again and aimed it at the rear end of the Chevy, where it had connected with the pickup. "Yer car looks like it might be okay, considerin'. Little bit of a gas leak–"

"Is Manny in the car, Clyde?"

" 'Course not," he answered, and shone the flashlight briefly into the car's interior. It was empty. "Why would he be in it, Sarah?" She didn't answer. He poked his head into the cab of the pickup: "Ground's hard, Sarah, but I think Manny coulda left some tracks. I'm gonna take a look. Yer stayin' here, right?"

"Can't you wait a minute, Clyde? Till there's some light."

"What if Manny's hurt, Sarah? The quicker I get to him the better. You'll be okay, here. Just lock the doors." He stepped away from the truck, walked to the front of the Chevy, looked back, heard Sarah open her door and scramble out. "Clyde?!" she called, "I'm coming with you, Clyde."

He aimed the flashlight at the front of the pickup. "Over here, Sarah."

She ran to him, and grabbed his arm: sudden fear had made her breathless. "It's . . . awful dark, Clyde. And cold."

"Not's cold as it was. Winter ain't on us yet." He

played the flashlight beam on a couple square yards of ground near the Chevy's driver's door.

"Clyde, that door don't work," Sarah told him.

He went around to the passenger side. He found Manny's footprints quickly and followed them off the road, Sarah still clinging to him.

Chapter 14

Norm Gellis closed the cellar window and locked it in one, quick, agitated motion. "Damn it!"

Marge came up behind him, rubbing her cheek. "I was just scared, Norm. That's why I was screaming. I was scared."

"Someone was *in* here, Marge. Someone was in here, and I shot at him, and I hit him." He paused to absorb it all; he squeezed the .38 affectionately. "I hit him, Marge," he repeated, as if in fascination.

"I'll call the sheriff, Norm." She turned quickly, with a sense of urgency, and started for the cellar stairs.

"You do, Marge, and you'll see that that little love tap I gave you was just the beginning. You understand me?"

She said nothing.

"And I told you to get something on, Marge. Unless you're going back to bed. Are you going back to bed, Marge?"

Still nothing. Her back was to him. She was motionless.

"I asked you a question, Marge."

"Yes," she answered.

"Yes what?"

"Yes, I'm going back to bed."

"You're not going to call that idiot sheriff?"

"No, I'm not, Norm." Her voice was steady, quiet, frightened. "I'm going right to bed, right now."

" 'Cuz he can't *do* nothin', Marge. All he can do is say, 'You got a permit for that .38?' and I'll have to tell him the truth, 'No, I don't, Mr. Sheriff,' and he'll say, 'Well then, I'm puttin' you under arrest.' Because all I wanta do, Marge, is protect my home and family and belongings, and the best way I know of doin' that is with this little beauty." He squeezed the gun again; he held it up, though Marge's back still was turned. "And you're sayin' you'd let him put me in *jail* for that, Marge? Mandatory *one year*?!"

"I'm not saying that, Norm. I just want to go back to bed. Can I do that?" she pleaded. "Can I go back to bed, Norm?"

"Sure you can." He lowered the gun and held it, barrel down, near his thigh. "But you ain't going to sleep, are you?"

"I'm pretty tired, Norm."

"I didn't ask you that."

She turned her head and futilely attempted a smile. "No, I'll stay awake. For you, Norm." And she moved slowly up the cellar stairs.

Norm glanced about. The cellar was filled with packing boxes and leftover building materials. He moved a yard to his right, peered over a large box filled with scraps of Fiberglas. He moved to the left.

"Shit!" he said. He had already completed what he supposed was a thorough search of the entire cellar and had found nothing. The trespasser, he felt certain, had escaped through the cellar window, because that's where the irregular trail of blood led.

He went to the stairs and glanced back. "Little punk!" he said, smiling, and he ascended the stairs quickly, his heavy footfalls covering the sound of the creature moving behind him, in a corner of the cellar where the light was dim.

The creature moved silently and swiftly to a nearby window. Beyond it, the warmth was returning. The creature reached up, slipped the window's lock, and pulled the window open.

In the kitchen just above, Norm Gellis paused and glanced confusedly at the floor. He hadn't heard movement so much as felt it, through the floor, with the soles of his feet. He shrugged. He'd searched thoroughly enough, and now there was Marge to deal with.

Chapter 15

Clyde straightened. He let the flashlight beam play on Manny Kent's face. "He's breathing okay, Sarah. *And* far's I can see, there ain't no blood."

"You think he hit his head?" Sarah asked, her voice quivering. She nodded to indicate the tall Empire fence only a couple feet from where Manny lay. "You think he tried to climb that fence and fell and hit his head?"

"I don't know what to think, Sarah." He aimed the flashlight at the fence, then at a spot just on the other side of it; something gleamed dully in the light. "You see that?"

Sarah nodded. "What is it?"

"It's the butt of my rifle."

"What's it doin' in there, Clyde?"

"I don't know what it's doin' in there. Manny'll tell us, soon's he comes around." He leaned over and put his hands under Manny's shoulders. He noticed, then, the slight, almost warm breeze moving around them. "You ready for some work, Sarah, 'cuz I can't carry him by myself, he's too damned big—"

"Clyde," Sarah cut in, her voice low. He looked up and saw her nod at the fence. "Clyde, someone's over there behind the fence."

He turned his head, looked; he saw nothing. "C'mon, Sarah," he said harshly, agitated. "Give me a hand." He pulled Manny to a sitting position. "I need your help—"

"Gimme the flashlight, Clyde. Someone's over there!"

"No there ain't, Sarah . . ."

In one fluid motion she pulled the flashlight from his pocket, aimed it at the fence and flicked it on.

Her scream made him stand bolt upright; it pushed adrenalin through his veins.

She screamed again and dropped the flashlight. She turned, ran.

Clyde turned his entire body very slowly, almost mechanically toward the fence.

He looked.

He saw nothing.

"And there ain't no blood," he heard. "Far's I can see." The illogic of his fear told him, *It's an echo, a kind of echo,* because the voice had been his voice: And then.

"What's it doin' in there, Clyde?" Sarah's voice.

"And there ain't no blood, far's I can see."

He saw movement. Shadows moving in the darkness beyond the fence. "Ba-na-na peels and mel-on rinds," he heard. "Ba-na-na peels and mel-on rinds." And the shadows and voices drifted slowly off, into the small stand of woods that crowded up to the fence.

He turned hurriedly back to his brother-in-law, lifted him, put him on his shoulders in a rough approximation of a fireman's carry. He didn't stop to wonder where his strength was coming from.

At the car, he put Manny down on the back seat. Sarah was in the front. "Shit!" she murmured. "Shit! It won't start. Shit!" Clyde looked. She was sitting stiffly in the driver's seat, both hands tight on the wheel. She couldn't be making an attempt to start the car, he realized, because she didn't have the keys.

"Sarah, are you okay?"

"Shit, it won't start!" she said again.

He pulled the keys from Manny's pants pockets, leaned over the back of the front seat, put his hands firmly on Sarah's shoulders. "Move over, Sarah—move over!" She let go of the steering wheel. "Shit, it won't start!" she said again.

"Move over, Sarah," he repeated, soothingly now. "We got to get outa here, Sarah."

She allowed him to slide her—with effort—to the passenger's side. He climbed to the front, put the key in the ignition. And noticed again the heavy, pervasive odor of gasoline. *Punctured gas tank,* he knew, and he hoped there was enough gas left in the tank to get them to a hospital.

He turned the ignition on and listened as the Sears Diehard cranked the engine frantically. He heard a heavy, muffled thumping noise from the back of the car; the car seemed to lift slightly at the same time. He checked the rearview mirror. What was all that light? he wondered. Was it sunrise, already?

*   *   *

The children moved as one away from the flames. They stopped quickly and, again as one, realized that there was no danger at this distance, only light, and warmth, just as the sun produced, and it delighted them.

But soon they felt pain, too. It arched toward them from within the car like a quickly moving red mist. And, still as one, they fled from it, away from the fence, to the various places within the stand of woods where they slept.

By sunrise, the fire was dead.

Chapter 16

From *The Penn Yann Post Gazette*, November 4:

VOLUNTEER FIRE CHIEF KILLED IN
FREAK ACCIDENT

Penn Yann Volunteer Fire Chief Clyde Watkins, 49, his sister, Sarah Kent, 40, and her husband, Manfred Kent, 43, all were killed early Saturday morning in what Police Chief John Hastings calls, "one of the weirdest and most tragic accidents I've seen in recent years." According to Hastings, a car driven by Watkins was traveling north on Sullivan's Road, a little-used gravel road off Route 43, 10 miles from Penn Yann, when it apparently sideswiped a pickup truck traveling in the same direction, and then burst into flames. The driver is thought to have been Mrs. Kent, whose body was found between the truck and the car. Manfred Kent's body was found in the back seat of the car. According to Hastings, "After the accident, Mrs. Kent may have left the pickup truck to help her brother and her husband, then was overcome by the intense heat and smoke."

All three bodies were very badly burned. Identification of Watkins and of Manfred Kent had to be accomplished from dental records.

Clyde Watkins lived all his life in Penn Yann. After graduating from the Penn Yann Central High School he served six years in the Marine Corps . . .

Janice McIntyre thought this would be the last warm day of the year. She checked the outdoor thermometer, under the kitchen window; sixty-eight degrees. She tapped it. Sixty-eight degrees. Amazing, November fourth and sixty-eight degrees. She was glad she'd gotten out of the house. She wondered if there was anything she could do in the yard this fine warm day. She remembered seeing Trudy Wentis trimming her rose bushes a couple weeks earlier and she wondered if dogwood trees needing trimming before winter. It was a frivolous idea, she thought.

She decided then to get a lawn chair from the little tool shed at the back of the yard. She crossed the yard quickly, opened the tool shed door, scanned the inside. No lawn chairs. A riding mower, hedge clippers, a can of turpentine, but no lawn chairs. She remembered—the lawn chairs were in the cellar. "Best to keep the vinyl away from sub-zero temperatures," Miles had explained. Good, practical, understanding Miles.

She closed the tool shed door. She started for the house.

She stopped. Her breathing stopped. She heard

a scream begin in a remote corner of her consciousness, where her fears lived.

The tall, dark-haired woman in the second floor
window—their bedroom—was shaking her head
slowly. *No*, she was saying. *No!*

Janice felt the scream inside her begin to change,
to metamorphize. And when, at last, it settled in
her throat, and vaulted from her mouth, it became,
"Who *are* you?! Who *are* you?!"

And the woman vanished.

"Hello."

"Mr. Marsh?"

"Yes, this is John Marsh."

"You don't know me, Mr. Marsh. My name is
Janice McIntyre. The editor of the local paper gave
me your number."

"Yes?"

"I called him for some information about a fire
that happened out here about fifteen years ago."

" 'Out here'?"

"Yes, Granada. That's the new housing development—"

"I know what it is, Mrs. McIntyre. You're calling
about the fire at the Griffin house, aren't you?"

"Yes, I am. Actually, I'm calling about Mrs.
Griffin."

"Rachel?"

"Yes."

"Why would you call about her, Mrs. McIntyre?
She died in that fire. So did her husband."

"I know that, Mr. Marsh. I've seen the newspaper
story. But what I really need to know—"

"Fifteen years, Mrs. McIntyre. Why don't we let
them rest?"

"Could you describe her, Mr. Marsh? Could you describe Rachel Griffin for me?"

"Describe her? What in the hell for, Mrs. McIntyre?"

"I know it seems odd, Mr. Marsh, but—"

"It seems kind of perverse, Mrs. McIntyre. Doesn't it seem kind of perverse?"

"Mr. Marsh, please try to understand. I've seen a woman around here. I've seen her *in* my house—"

"*Rest*, Mrs. McIntyre—that's what Rachel Griffin needs. Rest." And he hung up.

Janice had been using the kitchen phone; she glanced now, uneasily, at the little breakfast nook. "Rachel?" she whispered. "Are you trying to tell me something, Rachel?"

She waited silently for only a few seconds. Then, in fear of an answer, she fled the house.

Fifteen Years Earlier

Even as she struggled out of sleep, Rachel knew the source of the acrid smell that filled her nostrils. She nudged Paul, asleep beside her. "Paul," she said aloud. "Wake up, Paul."

"It's too cold," he groaned.

She shook him. "Paul, wake up!"

He opened his eyes, raised his head a little. "What's wrong? What's that smell?" He sat up suddenly. "My God . . ." He swung his feet to the floor, stood, grabbed the doorknob tightly, yanked his hand back. He cursed.

Rachel scrambled out of bed.

"The doorknob's hot." Paul's voice was trembling. "It's the house, Rachel! It's on fire!"

Chapter 17

Timmy Meade stroked the big, short-haired gray cat delicately, uncertain what its reaction might be. "Hi there, kitty cat. You got a name?"

The cat purred loudly, then lay down and rolled to its back, exposing its belly.

Timmy winced. Coagulated blood matted the cat's fur around the bottom of its rib cage. "Shit damn, cat!" He touched the long, narrow wound gently; it seemed fresh. The cat rolled away from his hand.

"Mom!" he called, turning his head toward the house. "Mom!"

Dora Meade appeared behind a sliding glass door. She pushed the door open slightly. "What is it?" she called.

"I got this cat out here, Mom, and it's hurt."

"Cat? What cat?" She opened the door and stepped out to the patio, where her son and the cat were. "That's a stray, Timmy." She made pushing motions in the air above the cat. "Shoo!" The cat continued to purr. "Shoo!" she repeated, and she prodded at it with her foot.

"It's hurt, Mom!" her son protested.

"It's a stray, Timothy, and it's probably diseased." She prodded it harder; the cat flipped suddenly to its feet, swiped at her ankle, and, moments later, vanished into the tall weeds at the perimeter of the yard.

At the same time—In the small stand of woods west of Granada

"You hear 'em?" said Robin Graham quietly.

"Yeah," said his twin brother, Robert. "I hear 'em."

They were on a deer path, although, as they had agreed, it was really a path which had been made by "red Indians" who "for sure were watchin' and waitin' and you gotta be gosh darn extra awful careful 'round those red Indians." They had played the game for years, first in the hallways and elevators of their apartment building in Rochester, New York—before they'd started going to school—then on the railroad tracks, between parked railway cars, near their second home in Albany, then in the abandoned gravel pits just a mile from their third home in Webster, New York. This, they agreed, was by far the very best place to play the game. And so what if maybe they were getting a little too old for kids' games. Because here, in these woods, maybe there really were red Indians. There was something, sure enough. Something that moved, and laughed, and repeated the things you said. Like an echo. Make a noise like a red Indian and, presto, there it was, all around.

And sometimes, if you looked close enough, you could actually see them. If you blinked just right, or moved your head just right, there they were. For a second. Or a half second. The red Indians on the run. Whoopin' and hollerin' and gigglin'.

"I bet she's here somewhere," Robin said.

"Bet who's here?" Robert asked.

"The one I seen the other night. The one with the nice little boobs."

And the way the woods closed up around you, you could almost believe you'd gone back a thousand years, because there was no sky with jet trails in it, and no houses and no cars—only the trees, and the dark, and the red Indians all around.

"You remember," Robin said. "I told you about her."

"I remember," Robert said.

"I'm gonna go lookin' for her tonight."

"No you ain't."

"I sure am. When you're asleep, so you can't tell Mom." He was whispering.

"I'll stay awake then. All night long." Robert was whispering, too.

"You do and I'll tell Mom about that magazine you got."

"What magazine?"

"You know what magazine."

"I burned that up. It was dumb."

"That's a lie."

"No it ain't."

"Quiet!"

"Don't tell *me* to be quiet!"

Robin clamped his hand over his brother's mouth. "I said be quiet! Listen!" He slowly took his hand away from Robert's mouth. "Listen," he repeated. "Can'tcha hear?"

"Hear what?"

"The red Indians. They're gone."

Robert listened a long while. "Yeah," he said at last, wonderingly. "They are. Where'd they go, you think?"

"I don't know." Robin sounded annoyed. "You think I can read minds or somethin'?" He started down the path that would take him out of the woods. Robert stayed put. Robin stopped, looked back. His mouth fell open, his eyes widened.

Robert said, "Robin, what's wrong?"

Robin gulped theatrically. "Jees, Robert—I seen her again, right there." He nodded at an area a couple feet to the right of where his brother was standing. "And she was just like before, Robert. Just like before. Naked! Jees, Robert, didn'tcha see her, didn'tcha see her?"

Robert grimaced. "I didn't see nothin', you're full of it!" and he glanced uneasily to his right, said, "You're full of it!" again, to which his brother made no reply, and moved quickly down the path and out of the woods.

Robin followed a half hour later.

Marge Gellis watched the pen shiver in her hand. She set the pen down next to the sheet of yellow stationery. The sheet was blank. It would stay blank, she realized, because whatever courage, or conviction, she ever possessed had left her long ago (the day she and Norm were married, she knew). And it wasn't as if she had any place to go, any money, or friends, or relatives who could take her in. (Her mother, in that lousy, two-room apartment, certainly wouldn't welcome her, she knew.)

She was probably very fortunate that she had this place, and Norm; at the age of forty-five and never having been attractive, anyway, and with no talents, she was caught here, and lucky for it.

She worked the piece of yellow stationery into her hand, as if her hand were a spider gobbling the paper up. She wadded the paper into a tight ball and held it in her fist for a long while.

To have used it, she thought, to have written the kind of letter to her husband that her impulses told her had to be written would surely have been an act of self-destruction.

Chapter 18

Trudy Wentis wondered if it might, after all, have been a mistake to bring Sam back here, despite what the omniscient doctor had told her and Dick. ("It may act as a spur to his eventual recovery. It's where he was found, you know, and there are memories locked up inside him, memories that can't help but crowd back. And, as well, this sort of thing—the abandonment of a child, and he was, obviously, abandoned, is something we don't like to see set aside. If at all possible, we like to see the parents brought to justice, in time. Sam can help us do that.") Because "justice" was fine, and noble, but not at the expense of a child's peace of mind. That price was too high.

She watched him. He was at the edge of the yard, his back to her; he was very still, and quiet, his eyes apparently on the dark, thick line of woods a half mile off. She pitied him suddenly for the turmoil at work inside him, the forces pulling and pushing him this way and that, and she pitied herself, too, because she had no idea what those forces were, where they originated, or why, and therefore could not help him very much; and, as a consequence, could not help herself.

"Sam?" she called. He did not turn to answer. He said nothing. "Sam, your lunch is ready." There was no response.

Evening

Malcolm Harris tossed the just-used fireplace match into the fire; he stretched his six-and-a-half-foot frame out in front of the fireplace. "Did she go back to sleep okay?" he asked his wife, Shelly, as she came into the living room from their seven-month-old daughter's bedroom, on the second floor. "Or did you have to shove a tit in her mouth?" he went on, and chuckled a little. (He had tried to talk his wife out of breastfeeding; "I know it was all the rage years ago, Shell, but, my God, times change.")

Shelly chose not to respond directly to his remark. "I had to put her on her stomach," she said. "She was on her back. She's fine, Malcolm."

" '*Malcolm*'?" He grimaced, glanced around at her. "Okay—'breast.' Is that better?"

She smiled slightly. *Not really*, the smile said. She nodded at the fireplace, at the fire Malcolm had built. It was crackling and pulsing nicely. "May I join you?" she said.

He got into a sitting position, patted the floor beside him. "Please do."

She sat beside him, her legs straight, arms behind her, palms flat on the floor. "Do you like it here?" she asked.

"I like it here. Yes."

"Enough for a long-term commitment?"

"How long-term?"

"Oh, I don't know. Until Serena's grown."

"That's a long time, Shell."

"Sure it is. But she needs the security and the stability—we all do."

Malcolm smiled; he had heard the "security and stability" lecture before. He put his arm around her, pulled her to him, kissed her: "Let's make love," he said.

"Yes," she whispered.

Robin Graham listened a full five minutes to his twin brother's deep, slow breathing. When, at last, he had convinced himself that Robert was asleep, he got out of bed and crossed to the closet. He put his hand on the doorknob.

"I'll tell Mom," Robert said. "If you go anywhere I'll get up and go in her bedroom and tell her."

"I was just going to go to the bathroom," Robin said immediately, and he moved quickly to the bedroom door; he opened it.

"I really will," Robert said. "I mean it."

"I know you *mean* it," Robin said. "And I think you're just jealous."

Robert thought for a moment about that. He lifted his head from the pillow. "Why would I be jealous? I ain't got nothin' to be jealous of, 'cuz yer just *hallucinatin'!*"

"I'm what?"

"Hallucinatin'. That means you're seeing things that ain't there—like naked people in the bushes. Whatsa matter, you didn't listen to Mr. Armstrong in English today—"

But Robin had left the room.

Robert heard the bathroom door close hard, the lock falling into place. Robin would probably spend a good long time in there, he thought. He'd probably whack off or something, thinking about what he saw.

Robert laid his head back on the pillow. Sleep came more quickly to him than he had wanted or supposed it could.

"I'm going to have to cure you of this," said Malcolm Harris.

"Cure me of what?" Shelly asked, sitting up in the bed beside him. She got a pack of Larks from the nightstand, lit one. "Smoking?"

Malcolm smiled quickly. "That, too. No, I mean your lack of adventurousness."

"Adventurousness?"

"Sure." He paused; her cigarette smelled good; he wished, briefly, that he hadn't quit. "Like—where did we just make love?"

"Huh?"

"*Where* did we just make love? Here, right? In this bed. In this bedroom. And where do you think I *wanted* to make love?"

She grinned. "In the refrigerator?"

He let his head fall back against the headboard; he rolled his eyes as if in exasperation. "Lord Jehovah, *Gott in Himmel*. No, no, Shelly. Not in the refrigerator. Downstairs! In front of that beautiful fire! That's why I made it, so we could make love in front of it. That's called being adventurous."

"Uh-huh. It's also called a good way to catch pneumonia. It's *cold* down there, Mal."

"Shelly, darling," he began, using his most patronizing tone, "that's why I built the fire."

She got out of bed, pulled the blanket from it suddenly, wrapped the blanket tightly around her:

"Hey!" Malcolm protested, quickly covering himself with the top sheet.

"See, it *is* cold, isn't it?" Shelly said, grinning, and she left the room.

The brown suede jacket Robin Graham wore (his mother had stitched his name in green yarn near the cuff of the left-hand sleeve) and the blue jeans and sneakers were not quite enough to keep the cold out. He looked back at the house, shivered, took a deep breath. *What* was he doing, anyway? He had school in the morning and he had to get up at 5:30 and it was so cold out here and so warm in there, and if dumb Robert woke up and saw that he wasn't in bed and really did go and tell on him . . .

He walked quickly to the front of the yard, his anger building. Robert was always such a dud—a damned, dumb dud! Robin smiled at that. He turned his head and glared at the bedroom window: "Damned, dumb dud!" he whispered.

He turned left. He stopped after a couple of steps, momentarily disoriented. He looked at his house again, then at the Harris house next door, and across the street at a big yellow house (a grayish-cream color in the darkness) still in the final stages of construction. Where were the street lights? He turned around, looked across the little island—bordered by asphalt—on which his house, the Harris and Wentis houses, and several others not yet occupied, had been built. No street lights.

Just the frigid, still darkness, and, here and there, in some of the houses, a bathroom light left on for the night. The Wentises' backyard spotlight had been turned off, but he didn't notice this.

He squinted at the western horizon. The thick, dark line of woods a half mile off was barely discernible from a night sky that was clear and crowded with stars.

He took another deep breath.

Then, because he was eleven years old and healthy, and had seen something that had intrigued him—like a gift unopened—and because he hated his brother, but most of all because he was *alive*, and didn't need to think about it, he ran hard, breathing first through his nose and exhaling through his mouth, as he had been taught, and moving his arms with precision, and, with each step, pushing off with his toes, and all the while his eyes wide open, in wonderment, focused on the rapidly approaching, rapidly widening and broadening line of the forest in front of him.

Adventurousness be damned! Shelly Harris thought. Especially on a night like tonight.

She put her hand under the running bath water, found it was too hot, and turned the cold water faucet slightly:

She heard her husband's voice above the sound of the water. She went to the bathroom door. "Did you say something?"

Malcolm stuck his head out from their bedroom doorway. "Yes, I did. I wanted to know if you were downstairs just now."

"Downstairs? No. Why?" She wrapped the blanket more tightly around her.

"I heard something." He shrugged. "At least I thought I did." A pause. "Are you going to take a bath?"

"Uh-huh. What do you mean?—you heard something."

"Just a noise. It was nothing. Can I join you?"

"What kind of noise?"

He started toward her—naked—down the hallway. "Just a noise-noise, Shell. Now can I please–" He stopped, turned his head toward the stairway to his left; he looked puzzled.

Shelly called, "What's the matter?"

"There's someone downstairs," he answered quietly, incredulously. He held his hand up, as if to stop Shelly from leaving the bathroom, though she hadn't budged. "Stay there," he said, still quietly, but Shelly, the bath water running behind her, hadn't heard him.

"Malcolm?" she called, above the rushing noise of the water. She stepped out of the bathroom. "I can't hear what–" She stopped. Her eyes widened. ·

"Shelly?" said Malcolm. He followed her gaze to a spot about an arm's length away, on the stairs. "Shelly?" he said again, because he saw nothing on the stairs.

And something brushed against him very quickly. Hair, he thought, and the suggestion of a small, warm hand on his rib cage:

"What," he started, "in the name of heaven–"

"Damned, dumb, dud!" he heard. Once. Then again, and again, decreasing in volume down the hallway toward Serena's bedroom.

Malcolm saw the child then. At Serena's door. And the child's huge, pale blue eyes and exquisite mouth were blank, the body motionless, in soft profile, one hand on the doorknob and a dozen of the foot-long, strike-anywhere fireplace matches clutched tightly in the other.

Shelly screamed then—a scream of panic and desperation for her baby's sake. And a moment later, Malcolm felt her brush past him, her touch much the same as the child's had been.

And he watched, dumbfounded, unable to move, as she threw Serena's door open. He waited. Only moments. And she appeared again in the hallway, her daughter held tight in her arms. "She's okay, Malcolm. Thank God, oh thank God, she's okay!"

"Where . . . is he?" Malcolm said. But Shelly's thoughts were for Serena only. "Where in the hell *is* he?"

Chapter 19

From *The Penn Yann Post Gazette*, November 6:

SEARCH INTENSIFIED FOR MISSING
ELEVEN-YEAR-OLD BOY

Police Chief John Hastings has announced that the search for 11-year-old Robin Graham, missing since early Monday morning from his home in Granada, the new and exclusive development ten miles north of Penn Yann, has been intensified. Says Hastings, "We have requested and have been granted National Guard assistance, and will now be focusing our search with this additional manpower in an approximately 20-square-mile area around Granada, an area bounded by Tripp Road, Sullivan's Road, Route 43, and the Riley's Glen campsites."

Robin's mother, Lorraine Graham, reported her son missing on Monday morning, November 4, and although the search has, according to Hastings, been "extremely exhaustive," no trace of the boy has yet been found. Asked if the child might have been kidnapped, Hastings replied that "no ransom note has yet been received. We are keeping our lines of communication open."

According to Mrs. Graham, her son is probably wearing a brown suede jacket, with the name "Robin" sewn on the cuff, a red flannel shirt, blue jeans, and sneakers. Anyone having information regarding Robin's whereabouts is asked to contact Chief Hastings's office immediately. A reward of $5,000 has been posted for information leading to Robin's safe return.

Chapter 20

Norm Gellis looked up from his plate. "I got a theory, Marge." He pushed a forkful of meat loaf into his mouth. "About that little Graham kid."

"Yes?" Marge said. She forced herself to smile, as if intrigued. "What kind of theory?"

"A good one." He swallowed the meat loaf. "A good one," he repeated. He pointed with his fork at a bowl filled with baked potatoes. "Gimme one of those, would ya, Marge." She passed him the bowl, he took a potato, split it, lathered it up with margarine and sour cream. He looked critically at it. "There's a gang, Marge."

"A gang?" Marge said, and smiled again, more easily.

"That's right, Marge. A gang of kids. Country kids." He picked up the potato, held it in front of his mouth, angled it for the right position. "City kids have gangs, right? Why not"—he shoved the potato into his mouth—"country kids?" He nodded at the bowl of potatoes. "Gimme another one of those." She passed him the bowl.

"I always thought country kids would have better things to do, Norm." She smiled. "You don't think so?"

He harrumphed. "You tell me, Marge, what country kids got to do? Milk the cows? Naw—machines do all that. Slop the hogs? Naw—they keep the hogs in those great big pens, Marge, and they feed 'em automatically. I saw that on the news the other night. Whatsa matter, you don't watch the news? Mow the hay, pick the corn? Are you kiddin'? Machines do all that, and that's good, Marge. That's progress. But there's just one little problem, you see, and that problem is the country kids ain't got nothin' to do. Just like city kids ain't got nothin' to do. So, just like the city kids, the country kids get into these gangs."

"Gangs, Norm?"

"That's right. Like Hell's Angels, only minus the motorcycles, 'cuz they can't afford 'em." He grinned proudly. "And the way I see it, that's the problem we got out here, now, Marge." He poked the top of the table with his forefinger, for emphasis. "We got these country kids in a gang and they're fixin' to terrorize us. It's already started. Hell, it started a month ago, when that kid broke in here. And now this Graham boy turns up missing. And how about that kid who broke in here again, just a couple days ago?! How about him? And if you listen close, Marge, *real close*, to what some of the people are sayin' around here, you know it's happenin' to more than just us and that poor Graham woman. I heard that somethin' very strange happened at one of those new people's houses the other night." He paused to give Marge time to absorb what he was telling her. "So," he continued, "you know what I think, Marge? I think it's a kind of initiation, like a school initiation. That's why that kid we saw was *naked*. It's an initiation. I had one once. I belonged to this little club—you know, just a kid's club. And for our initiation we were sat down in front of two bottles, beer bottles. The quart size. And one, Marge, one had beer, okay. But the other one didn't." He grinned at her, as if to say, *You know what the other one had in it, don't you?* "And, anyway, we had to choose one of these bottles, and if we chose the wrong one, hey, that was too bad, 'cuz we had to drink the contents of the bottle we chose. Piss or beer, it didn't matter." He chuckled, remembering. "I chose the piss, wouldn'tcha know it." He chuckled again. "And that's what we got here, Marge. Some kind of initiation. Only it's gotten way outa hand. That's why they grabbed this Graham kid. Maybe he was parta the gang and he chickened out. Maybe he was nobody, just some kid they wanted to grab so they could make him part of the initiation proceedings. And if it has gotten *that* outa hand, Marge, then we're all in big trouble." He paused for some comment from Marge. She said nothing. She was smiling blankly. "Are you listening to me, Marge?"

"Yes, Norm."

"You agree with what I'm sayin'?"

"Yes, I do."

"Good, 'cuz I've come to the conclusion that steps have to be taken."

"Steps?"

"To meet these kids on their own ground, Marge.

To squash 'em good and hard, if that's what they're askin' for."

Lorraine Graham liked the buoyant feeling of separation that the Valium gave her. It was almost enough. She could almost forget the squads of pink-faced National Guardsmen, and the dogs, and the questions: "Would your son have any *reason* for leaving?" . . . "Has he run away before?" . . . "Has there been some squabble in the family?" . . . "Could we talk to your husband, please? . . . "I'm sorry; he's dead." . . . "Could your son be reacting to your husband's death, somehow?" . . . "Did he have a favorite place to go—a kid's hangout? . . . "No, we haven't lived here that long." . . . "Could you give us the names of some of his friends?" . . . "We haven't lived here that long. He and Robert stay pretty much to themselves."

Damn them all! This was a time for grief, didn't they know that? Robin was gone. Forever. He had walked out of the house in the middle of the night and had been swallowed up. Didn't they know that?!

"Mom?" It was Robert.

She lifted her head from the back of the easy chair, focused on him, said nothing.

"Mom?" he repeated.

"Yes?" she said quietly.

"They found Robin's jacket, Mom. Out in the woods, they wanted me to tell you."

She let her head fall back. "His jacket?"

"Yeah, Mom—the one he was wearing. The denim one."

She let her eyes close. "Oh. Yes. Are they going

to keep it—do they need it for evidence or something?"

"They didn't say they needed it, Mom. You want me to ask? I'll go back and ask if you want."

"Yes. Please. Go and ask."

"You okay, Mom?"

She said nothing.

"Mom, are you okay? You want me to get you something? I can make you some coffee, Mom. Or some tea."

Still nothing. She kept her eyes closed.

"Mom, are you okay?"

She opened her eyes; she focused on the ceiling. "Yes, Robin, I'm okay. Now please go and ask them about the jacket."

"I'm Robert, Mom."

"Just do as I say and go ask them if they're going to keep the jacket."

He hesitated, uncertain. At last he whispered, "Okay, Mom," and left hurriedly.

Lorraine closed her eyes again. Yes, she thought—Robin had surely been swallowed up. By this place around her; by the open sky, by the black, cold nights, by the quiet. It was fanciful, but it was true. Her favorite son had been swallowed up. Just like Stan had been swallowed up. Whole. And her mother, too.

Lorraine fingered the bottle of Valium on the table near her chair. She opened the bottle, put one of the pills on her tongue, and let her saliva work at it a moment.

Chapter 21

Janice McIntyre thought, *W.C. Fields*: The man at the door was the spitting image of W.C. Fields.

"Mrs. McIntyre?" he said.

"Yes, I'm Janice McIntyre." But, maybe on second thought—no. This man was too muscular, too weathered. "Can I help you?"

He lowered his head slightly, as if embarrassed. "We've never been introduced, Mrs. McIntyre, but we did talk on the phone the other day." He thrust his hand out awkwardly. Janice took it. "I'm John Marsh." He let go of her hand. "I'd like to talk to you."

She hesitated, momentarily uncertain, remembering his abrupt manner on the phone.

He nodded to indicate the confusion of National Guardsmen and sheriffs' deputies and the hubbub of voices and shouted commands and two-way radios in Granada that day. "I had a devil of a time getting in here."

"I'm sure you did, Mr. Marsh." Still uncertain.

"They ain't found that boy yet?"

"Not yet." She opened the door wide, stepped away from it. "Please, Mr. Marsh—come in."

He stared disconsolately at his cup of black coffee, then at Janice, seated across from him on the couch.

"Can I get you something else, Mr. Marsh? We have some fresh doughnuts."

"No thanks. Coffee's fine." He sipped it then, pointedly, set it down on the coffee table in front of the couch. The muscles on his face tightened, he took a deep breath, and said, his voice low, as if sharing some long-held secret, "Rachel Griffin was tall—maybe five foot nine or ten—and she was pretty. Not beautiful. Not like some Hollywood actress. But pretty. Nice to look at. And she wore her hair long, down to the middle of her back, far's I can remember. It was dark hair, almost black, but not quite." He paused just long enough to pick up his cup of coffee, as if that physical effort could steady him. "Is that who you seen around here, Mrs. McIntyre? You seen Rachel Griffin around here?"

Janice answered immediately, "Yes, that's who I've seen, Mr. Marsh."

"When?"

Janice closed her eyes for a moment; she felt her pulse quicken. "I've seen her twice. The last time was just a few days ago, and then, once before, during the first week of October." Her words came to her quickly, in a rush—perhaps, she thought, because she had someone to say them to, at last. "I think she's trying to tell me something, Mr. Marsh. Something about this house, about Granada. Maybe something about myself. I wish I knew. And I wish I knew something more about her than that she lived her last few months here, and that she died that way. In a fire. Because I think that's an awful way to die. I think it would *be* an awful way to die"—she smiled quickly, self-consciously—"Mr. Marsh. I wouldn't choose it, if I were given the choice." She realized she was on the verge of babbling. "So I want you to tell me more, if you can. I want you to tell me what kind of person she was and why she was living out *here*, for God's sake. It had to have been hell for her. I want you to help me to know her." She stopped suddenly, as if she had wound down. She felt a nervous smile play along her lips, and wished that Marsh would say something. She reached for her own cup of coffee, saw that her hand was shaking, clasped it in her other hand; she folded both hands in her lap. "Mr. Marsh, do you think I'm imagining things?"

He answered without hesitation. "I wouldn'ta come here if I thought that, Mrs. McIntyre."

The tension she had felt since his arrival dissipated suddenly. She sighed, lowered her head, closed her eyes.

"And no," Marsh went on. Janice raised her head slowly, opened her eyes. "It wasn't hell for her, Mrs. McIntyre. At least not at the beginning. The both of them—Paul and her—seemed to settle in pretty good here. They got the house cleaned up—" Janice looked questioningly at him. "Vandals had got into it, Mrs. McIntyre. It was a mess. I remember Paul Griffin blamed me a little for that. I was supposed to keep an eye on the house 'til they got here from New York. And I did keep an eye on it. Every day. And to this moment I can't figure out–" He paused; his voice had lowered considerably, he realized. He was talking more to himself than to Janice McIntyre. " 'Scuse me, Mrs. McIntyre. Going off into daydreams has got to be a habit of mine in my old age." Janice smiled slightly. Marsh continued, "I'd say Rachel and Paul were happy, considerin' all the problems. He wanted to be a farmer, you know. That was his dream. 'Course this land is too acid, now, and there ain't no top soil left no more . . . and Rachel—I think she just wanted to live here with him, come hell or high water."

"They had no children, Mr. Marsh?"

He hesitated a moment before answering; then, "There was some talk about a child out here. A man named Thompson did some work for 'em— fixed up some of their windows—and he swore to his dyin' day that when he came out here he heard children in the house. And around it. I heard things myself, if the truth be told. But that was before Rachel and Paul moved in."

"I'd say," Janice cut in, "that this man, Thompson, was right."

"Yer talkin' 'bout that pitiful little skeleton they found here, ain'tcha?"

She looked confusedly at him. "How did you . . . I mean, there's been nothing in the papers, Mr. Reynolds made sure of that–"

"Penn Yann's a small town, Mrs. McIntyre." He paused, as if that fact was explanation enough. "And I'll tell you somethin' else," he went on. "That skeleton's givin' the 'experts' a lota trouble. I hear they can't even tell what sex it is, and that's supposed to be easy. And I hear they can't tell for sure whether it's a little Indian child—maybe

Onondaga or Oneida Indian—or maybe a black child, or a white child, and they *think* it was layin' out here in the ground for a long, long time, but they don't know for sure—" He stopped. Janice's eyes were watering. He closed his mouth tightly, shook his head in self-condemnation. "Lord, I'm sorry, Mrs. McIntyre—"

She held her hand up. "No, forgive me, Mr. Marsh—there was no way you could have known. You see—" And she went on to tell him, painfully, and at length—as if, somehow, the telling was therapy for her—about Jodie. When she had finished, she quickly steered the conversation back to where it had begun: "What kind of woman was she?—Rachel, I mean. That's what I need to know, Mr. Marsh. That's what I desperately need to know."

He nodded slowly, solemnly. "Yes," he said, "I think you do." And he withdrew a small, white, unsealed envelope from his shirt pocket. He studied the envelope quietly for a long moment, as if there was something holy in it. Finally, he passed the envelope to Janice. She took it. He said, "I sent the original of this letter on to Rachel's mother, right after the fire, but I made this copy, first." He paused briefly, then explained, "Rachel and Paul Griffin were *special people*, Mrs. McIntyre. They had special dreams. And when that fire happened, when they died, I told myself I had to have a small piece of those dreams. We didn't find much, pokin' through the ashes of the house, but that was one thing we did find." He paused; Janice hadn't yet opened the envelope. "Go ahead," he coaxed. "You said you wanted to know Rachel Griffin. Read that letter and you'll know her's well as anyone."

She opened the envelope, withdrew the yellowed

Xerox copy, unfolded it, spread it out on her lap.
She read:

Dear Mother,

This will be my last letter before we see you
again. We'll be leaving in two days. I'd like to
explain everything to you here and now, sort
of get it all off my chest. But, to be truthful, I
don't believe I'll ever be able to *understand* it,
let alone explain it.

Are we running? Yes. That's a fair assess-
ment, I'd say. I can't tell you precisely what
we're running from; Paul's word for it is
"ghosts," and I don't think I could do any
better than that.

The important thing, the necessary thing,
for both of us, is that we *are* running. This is
going to sound terribly melodramatic, Mother, and you're going to ask me about it when I
see you, and I'm going to have to plead ignorance, but, if we don't run now, we won't be
able to run later. I'm sure of that. This is a
matter of survival.

I want to ask you a favor. When we get
back, when you see us again, please don't ask
any pointed questions. You'll be burning to
ask them, I know, and I'll be burning to
answer, but, well, both of us, Paul and I, have
a lot of questions to answer between ourselves first, and we've got a lot of time to
make up for, a lot of things to put behind
us.

For now, let me assure you that we are
both well, though a little tired—emotionally—

and that unless something unexpected happens we should see you within the week.

Paul sends his love. And so do I.

Rachel.

Janice found that her hands were shaking, that her eyes were watering again. The letter said so much, and it said so very little. It showed her Rachel's torment, and something of her hopes, and her humanness, and desperation.

Janice's gaze returned automatically to those cryptic phrases—"The important thing, the necessary thing, for both of us, is that we *are* running." . . . "This is a matter of survival." And to the shrill irony of that one word, "ghosts."

She reread the entire letter once. And again. And again. At last, she knew what Rachel had been telling her—what Rachel was trying to tell her even now.

"I'd like to be alone, Mr. Marsh," Janice said. She handed the letter and envelope back to him.

"Yes," Marsh answered quickly. "I understand." He stood, left the room. Janice listened as he got his coat from the coat tree near the door, listened as he put it on, and opened the front door.

"Mrs. McIntyre?" he called.

"Yes?"

"I've seen her, too," he said. And he left the house.

From *The Penn Yann Post Gazette*, November 15:

SEARCH HALTED FOR MISSING GRANADA BOY
The search for 11-year-old Robin Graham, missing since November 4 from his home at 26 Morningside Way, Granada, has been called

off, according to Penn Yann Police Chief John Hastings. "We have, with the aid of the National Guard, local, and state police, engaged in the most thorough and exhaustive search ever conducted in this county," Chief Hastings said. "And we must now, with deep regret, conclude that any further search would be futile." The case, however, Hastings continues, is "far from closed. It is entirely possible that Robin was picked up by a passing stranger, kidnapped, or even that he simply ran away from home and may soon show up again. No possibility is being left unexamined, and it is conceivable that, in time, this case will come to a happy conclusion."

The $5,000 reward for information leading to Robin's safe return has been increased, says Hastings, to $15,000. All leads will, upon request, be kept strictly confidential.

Chapter 22

The creature had fallen seventy feet to the bare earth from the upper branches of an aged honey locust. The creature had climbed the honey locust for no other reason than it *could* climb it; and it had fallen because it knew nothing about old trees and decayed branches. It knew only about itself—what pain was, and what cold was—and how to protect itself from the cold—and it knew about heat, and hunger, and about desire. It knew what the earth said it must know.

The creature did not know it was dying. Since its birth only weeks before, it had killed, and it had seen death, and it had experienced life. But it could not give names or meanings to anything—its brain was not set up for clutter.

The fall from the honey locust—which would not have been fatal had the creature jumped instead of fallen wildly out of control—had broken the creature's back. One lower rib, as well, had pierced its heart. And so it was dying. Very painfully and slowly.

Its eyes followed the subtly changing patterns of light and shadow all around. That changing pattern was what it had first seen, weeks before, when the earth was done giving it life.

The creature could not smile. If it were human, it might. But it wasn't. So, blankly, it watched the changing patterns of light and shadow; it experienced the pain. And, in time, life stopped within it.

Forever.

The new creature pushed itself up to a half-sitting position. It stood. It felt the soft creepers of the hard wind that was pushing the tops of the trees about; it heard the busy, quick noises of squirrels and rabbits and raccoons, and a thousand others, making ready for the winter. It saw the changing patterns of light and shadow all around.

And it felt its muscles moving gracefully over its bones; the air swelling its lungs:

The others present at the birth touched and prodded the creature. Wonderingly. Because the creature was alive, and warm. As they were. And because they could see. And hear. And taste. And smell. And also touch.

Because they had sprung from the earth. And were alive.

Lorraine Graham thought she recognized the man, though, in her Valium-induced fog, she wasn't sure. "Yes?" she said, being certain to keep the door open only a couple inches.

"Hi," the man said. "I'm Norm Gellis. I live in back of you." He nodded to indicate his house.

"Hello, Mr. Gellis."

"Hi," he said again, obviously nervous. "I thought we could have a talk, Mrs. Graham."

"I don't know if I'm up to a talk, Mr. Gellis." She began to close the door.

"It's about your son, Mrs. Graham."

The door was open only a crack; Lorraine held it there. "My son is gone," she said.

"Why? Because they couldn't find him? I think he's still alive, Mrs. Graham."

"Why would you think that, Mr. Gellis?"

"Why would you say he's dead?"

"I didn't say that. I said he was gone."

"Which is my point exactly, Mrs. Graham—"

"He's been swallowed up, Mr. Gellis. This place just . . . swallowed him up." Her tone was one of resignation; her voice cracked as she spoke. "It'll swallow us all up, Mr. Gellis. You, me, everybody—"

"I got a theory, Mrs. Graham—"

"He was a good boy, Mr. Gellis. Not a saint. But a pretty good boy. And he was very bright."

"You see, Mrs. Graham, the country kids got this gang—sorta like Hell's Angels, only without the motorcycles—"

"*Too* bright, really." Her mood had become contemplative. "That's why he was swallowed up. Because he wasn't about to stay close to home with me, as he should have—"

"And these kids, this gang of kids, these country kids, Mrs. Graham, are set to terrorize the whole community—"

"My husband was swallowed up, too."

"And it's up to each and every one of us to fight

them, Mrs. Graham. These are our homes, Mrs. Graham." He had practiced this speech and, listening to himself now, he thought it sounded good. "It's where our children will grow tall." He wondered, briefly, if that was inappropriate; he went on, "It's a place we must *protect*–"

"Stan was swallowed up by a heart attack, Mr. Gellis. My mother was swallowed up by a stroke. It's the same sort of thing. It has to do with the blood. It all has to do with the blood." And she slowly closed the door. "Goodbye, Mr. Gellis," she said, when the door was closed and she was making her way into the living room.

Robert Graham wished the kid in the seat behind him would shut up. He wished Timmy Meade and Sam Wentis hadn't stayed after school to play soccer. He wished the bus driver would slow down, and he wished he didn't have an erection (why in hell did he always get an erection just before he got off the bus?); and that he didn't have to go home and watch his mother wander around the house like some freakin' zombie. But most of all, he wished his brother was in the seat beside him, jabbing him in the ribs, making an ass of himself, being a general pain in the butt. But *here*, anyway. With him. In the bus. Not out there. Lost. In the cold!

And he wished he could stop crying. "You *cryin'*, Robert?!" he heard, followed by a burst of giggling. "Don't *cry*, Robert."

"You shut up," Robert said.

"What'd you say, Robert? I can't *hear* you."

Robert turned his head very slowly and stiffly.

The boy behind him was two years older and twenty pounds heavier and he was grinning a challenge.

Robert felt the anger welling up inside him, felt his eyes narrow and his mouth tighten, felt his hands clench into fists. He hissed, "You shut up or I'll knock your fuckin' teeth outa your fuckin' ugly head!"

The older boy's grin froze. Then, slowly, it dissipated. "Okay," the boy said, his voice trembling slightly. "Okay, don't get all bent outa shape!"

Robert turned his head back. The anger was still with him. It was, in fact, building.

The bus driver, a man nicknamed Hog (because he looked something like a hog), glanced at the speedometer; it read 50. He thought about slowing down, then decided his driving skills were more than a match for Reynolds Road, narrow as it was, and rough as it was. (*A year,* he remembered; everyone said the road would be widened and paved in a year. In the meantime, it was sure going to be a hell of a winter.)

He checked the rearview mirror. Jesus H. Christ! The Graham kid was crying again. Damn, they just didn't build kids the way they used to. Of course, take the kid away from his mother and he'd straighten around in no time; better a boy had a father and no mother than the other fucking way around.

He looked back at the road:

Jesus Damn! he thought frantically. *I already been through this turn, ain't I?*

And he hit the brake pedal hard; the brakes caught; the bus started sliding to the left, off the road:

Get your foot off the brake, asshole! he thought then. *You get your license from a Sears Catalogue?* And he found that panic had riveted his foot to the pedal.

The bus shimmied to the right, as if doing a huge, awkward two-step. The front sideswiped an oak just off the road, at the edge of an embankment halfway through the turn.

Hog screamed abruptly.

The back of the bus swung around 180 degrees and, for a split second, the bus hung motionless at the edge of the road. Then it flipped once and slid, on its side, down the embankment. It stopped within moments, held in place by the front edges of a small stand of white birch trees.

Hog lay with his belly on the steering wheel, his face mashed against the side window. He was dimly aware that he was urinating spontaneously and he hoped the kids in the bus couldn't see that. "Okay," he grunted, though his voice was barely audible, even to himself, "everyone stays calm, right?—'cuz everything's gonna be A-okay if we just–" And he died.

Trudy Wentis made an effort to look as if she were actually thinking over what Janice McIntyre had just told her, that she hadn't merely rejected it out of hand. She wondered how convincing she was. Janice pursed her lips and shook her head slowly—Trudy realized she hadn't been very successful at all. "Damn!" she said. "I'm sorry."

"Me, too," Janice said. She shook her head more quickly and smiled a small, self-condemning smile. "I really didn't expect you to accept any of that, but it was good to let it come out."

They were in Janice's living room, Janice in a huge, oval-backed, brown wicker chair —she looked very small in it—and Trudy across from her on a dark, oriental-print love seat. Trudy leaned forward in the love seat and said, as if repeating a confidence, "And you've already asked Miles about leaving Granada?"

"Yes, I have. He says, 'Let's wait and see,' and that's fair enough. I mean, what reasons can I give him?—'Hey, Miles, there's this ghost that's trying to tell us to leave'?" She harrumphed. "I can't say that."

"Then what did you tell him?"

Janice waved at the air as if waving away a bothersome insect. "I don't know—something about being pregnant and maybe it'd be better if we lived closer to the city."

"That's plausible, anyway."

"More plausible than a ghost in the breakfast nook, you mean?"

Trudy sat back in the love seat. "Yes," she said without hesitation. "More plausible than that."

The doorbell rang.

Janice pushed herself out of the big, wicker chair; she looked Trudy squarely in the eye: "You're a good friend," she said. "You don't lie to me. I like that."

"I try not to lie to anybody, Janice."

Robert Graham sat down hard on the embankment and studied the dark underside of the overturned bus for a long while. *Jees,* he thought, *what is all that stuff?* He knew, from mechanics class, what the transmission was, and the drive shaft, and the muffler and tailpipe. But there was so much other stuff, too—wires and springs and little iron wheels. What was it all for?

He looked about. To his right, the embankment gave way to gnarled underbrush. To his left, erosion had begun—the result of poor drainage from the road bed—and there were twenty yards or so of bare, red soil. Close to him, the heavy, sliding bus had gouged into the dark brown clay just inches beneath.

He shivered and, for the first time, wondered how, exactly, he'd gotten out of the bus, and what he was doing here, in back of it. He had a fleeting glimpse of kicking the emergency window open and pulling himself out. That glimpse showed him Hog's body, as well, and the folded-up body of the smart-assed kid behind him. And he thought, obliquely, that they were both probably dead, though not the little girl in front, he realized. Because he could hear her crying even now.

The "right thing" (a phrase, he remembered wistfully, that his mother had often used) would probably be to go back inside the bus and help that poor little girl somehow. Pull her out the same window he'd come out of, maybe. Or make sure she was comfortable. Not too badly hurt. Or, if she *was* hurt, to soothe her. That would be the "right thing."

He stood. "Hey, little girl in the bus," he called, hands cupped around his mouth. "Hey, little girl there in the bus!"

He heard her crying slowly stop. She called back, "My name is *Loretta!*" as if being called "little girl" offended her.

"Yeah, Loretta. Are you hurt bad?"

Silence.

"Loretta, I said are you hurt bad?"

"No. I don't know. I cut my finger on something. On the seat, I think. I cut my finger on the seat."

"Is your finger bleeding?"

Silence again.

"I said is your finger bleeding, Loretta?"

"*I* don't know. You think I wanta *look* at it?"

"Jesus!" Robert whispered. "Loretta?" he called. "I'm going away now. I'm going to go and find Robin." He started around the front of the bus, through the twenty-yard slice of erosion.

Loretta called shrilly, "Who's Robin?"

Robert called back, "He's my brother," and his tone lowered, became smooth and conversational. "My twin brother." He smiled. "Yeah. I'm gonna find him." He called. "I won't be a minute. You stay there, Loretta."

"Don't go away," Loretta pleaded. "Oh, please don't go away! There's something wrong with the bus driver. What's wrong with the bus driver?! Oh *please* don't go away!"

Robert made his way quickly around the front of the bus, his arms high to balance himself on the eroded embankment.

"And so," Norm Gellis explained; he had seated himself next to Trudy Wentis on the love seat. "My theory is—there's a gang. A gang of country kids. And these kids"—his head bobbed as he talked, caught up as he was in what he was saying, and his wide-eyed gaze flitted from Trudy to Janice— "have got this initiation. Like an initiation in school. And a part of this initiation is to terrorize us. All of us."

"In what way?" Janice asked.

"Ha!" he exclaimed, and he jabbed at the air with his forefinger for emphasis, "that's where they've got us, because, up till they snatched the Graham kid all they did was diddly-shit stuff—pardon my French. You know, runnin' 'round naked, tryin' to scare the daylights outa people. Diddly-shit stuff. But when they snatched the Graham kid, hell, that was a declaration of war! No doubt about it!"

"You think the Graham boy was kidnapped, Mr. Gellis?" Trudy asked, turning her head slightly to hide her flickering, nervous smile. "Why would someone kidnap him?"

Norm Gellis looked as if the question had taken him by surprise. "Hey," he said, "you think *I* should know? You think *I* can get inside these kids' heads?" He paused and looked from Janice to Trudy. "Huh?" he went on. Both women stayed quiet. He was vaguely aware that they both seemed very ill at ease. He continued, "I'll tell ya—I was a security agent at a kids' detention home for 25 years before I retired." Which was partially true; he had been a security agent for six months, many years before, until being fired; cruelty was alleged, but not proven. "And I seen all kindsa kids—kids that'd stab you in the back for your last quarter, and I could never figure out one of 'em. Not a one. And you want me to get inside the heads of these kids around here?! Fat chance. *You* go and try. All I'm doin' is sounding the alarm, that's all—just sounding the alarm!"

Janice stood abruptly. She smiled stiffly and stuck her hand out. Norm Gellis stood unsteadily and took her hand. She said, "Well, you *have* warned us, haven't you?!" She let go of his hand and nodded at the front door. "Thank you, Mr. Gellis."

He looked stunned. "Don't you wanta know what we should do? About these kids, I mean. I've worked it all out and I was thinking I could come back later, when your husbands are home, and we could all sit down and talk about it."

"My husband's going to be working late, Mr. Gellis," Janice said, the stiff smile still on her lips. "Every night this week, in fact."

He turned to Trudy: "And how about you? Is your husband going to be busy, too?"

"My husband's always busy, Mr. Gellis."

He stared at her a few moments; then, "We got a problem here, a big *problem*, and you *females* just sit around *laughing* about it!"

"Mr. Gellis," Janice said, "we really are not laughing at you—"

"Shit on that!" he cut in, and he moved quickly to the living room entranceway. He turned back: "Laugh!" he hissed. "Go ahead! You're all gonna *die* laughing!"

A moment later, he had slammed the front door behind him.

Chapter 23

Evening came quickly. It erased the green of evergreens, the yellows and reds of deciduous trees and autumn flowers, and transformed all of it to gray and black—a fuzzy and aged daguerreotype come to life. Except in Granada itself, thanks to the street lamps, and spotlights, and the blaze of lights in the houses.

No one had yet discovered the overturned bus, though several had passed it—Miles McIntyre, on his way home, Dick Wentis and Larry Meade, also on their way home. (Malcolm Harris had come down with a slight fever shortly after waking that morning and so had not gone to work.) They had missed seeing the bus for several reasons: the darkness, most importantly, and the fact that it lay a full fifty feet down the embankment and could only be seen by someone actually walking on the edge of the road. And exhausted, anyway, from a day's work, and in need of being home, each man had even failed to see the telltale skid marks on the soft shoulder.

Inside the bus, rigor mortis had stiffened Hog up; it would begin to fade by daybreak.

Just behind him, fifteen-year-old Eric Miller, Robert's tormentor, lay confused and in pain, and very hungry. He had suffered a slight concussion and a fractured wrist in the accident—and the resulting fall from his seat to where he now lay—and, for the three hours since, had been utterly afraid to move or speak.

At the middle of the bus, Loretta sat on a window, her feet against the bus roof, and sucked her thumb hard; the thumb had become shriveled and white. Every fifteen minutes or so she took it from her mouth and called angrily, her voice quaking, "You ... You ..." and then stuck her thumb back into her mouth.

Robert Graham sat up straight against the Empire fence, his legs outstretched, his hands folded on his thighs. He had come to realize, dimly and reluctantly, that his search for Robin was at an end, and he felt guilty for it, as if weak and unworthy; Robin would not have ended the search so quickly. He'd have looked until morning, for sure, maybe even until afternoon, because he was strong and heroic.

"Fuck you, Robin!" Robert said, and smiled uneasily, as if he had swallowed an odd kind of poison that was soothing him first.

And in the darkness, he felt something sit beside him against the fence and touch him, shoulder to shoulder. An elbow poked hard into his rib cage. "I don't know," he heard. "I guess she was thirteen or fourteen. And she had these great little boobs, like Mom has."

Robert turned his head very slowly, in stark disbelief. The face in profile beside him was little more than a pale half-oval. "Mom . . . is going to be . . . worried about us, Robin," he said haltingly, for lack of anything better to say.

"Get home, then."

"I can't." This was a trick! Some kind of trick! This wasn't Robin beside him. It couldn't be Robin! "Not unless you come with me."

Silence.

"She's taking those stupid pills, Robin."

"Those stupid pills."

"She takes them all the time. She walks around like she's made of butter, like she's a freakin' zombie!"

"A freakin' zombie."

"Yeah, Robin. She'll stop taking them if you come home." But it *was* Robin beside him. Jesus, it was, it *had* to be!

"Like she's made of butter."

"Bones and everything, Robin."

"Yeah. A freakin' zombie. Like she's made of butter."

"She misses you real bad. Come on home, why don'tcha?"

"Little boobs, just like Mom has." The voice changed pitch suddenly and became a woman's voice. "I can't do that, Clyde."

A game, Robert decided. Sure. This was a game. "Can't do what, Robin?" He smiled tentatively—games were supposed to make you smile.

"I can't go prowlin' 'round out there in the pitch dark."

"Then we'll wait till the sun comes up. We'll wait right here."

Silence.

"Okay?"

"Right here."

"Uh-huh, till the sun comes up."

"Till the sun comes up. Right here. Uh-huh."

"Robin?"

The creature's hand moved very quickly in the darkness. Hunger moved it, and desperation. Its fingers touched Robert's windpipe, very gently at first, as if in a caress; and it *was* a caress, a kind of thank you from one creature to another for the gift of itself.

Then the creature's fingers stiffened and came together on Robert's windpipe. Robert made several small, dry, hacking noises.

And felt great surprise that death could happen so easily and so quickly, like spilling a glass of milk at dinner. He had supposed that huge black clouds should have formed at the horizon, and that sad music should have been playing for days beforehand. At least in his head.

From *The Rochester Democrat and Chronicle*, November 25:

ONE DEAD, TWO HURT, ONE MISSING IN BUS CRASH

One man is dead, two children are hurt, and one child is missing following the crash Thursday of a Penn Yann school bus.

The bus, driven by Howard Welsh, 43, the dead man, was apparently traveling north on Reynolds Road, approximately ten miles north of Penn Yann, some time late Thursday afternoon, when it skidded, flipped over, and careened down an embankment. Mr. Welsh was killed instantly. One of the two injured children, Eric Miller, 15, of Bergen, New York, is still under observation at Myers Community Hospital in Penn Yann, with head wounds and a broken wrist. The other child, Loretta Marks, whose address was given as R.D. 4, Penn Yann, was treated for minor cuts and released.

The missing child, Robert Graham, 13, a resident of Granada—New York City entrepreneur Rowland Reynolds's newly built housing development near Penn Yann—apparently escaped from the bus through an emergency window shortly after the accident and wandered into the surrounding woods in search of his twin brother, Robin, who has been missing since November 15th. According to Penn Yann police, a thorough search is now being made for Robert, who is described as 5'5" tall, with short brown hair, brown eyes, and wearing tan corduroy pants and a green pullover sweater.

There is evidence that excessive speed may have contributed to the accident, according to Sharon Jarvis, media liaison for the Penn Yann police. Says Ms. Jarvis, "Skid marks and other evidence at the scene indicate strongly that Mr. Welsh may have been proceeding down Reynolds Road at a speed which was improper for road conditions and which may have markedly contributed . . ."

Chapter 24

December 5

Norm Gellis lifted his head slightly from the pillow and peered into the adjoining bathroom. Marge was sure taking a hell of a long time in there this morning. Christ, did she think she owned it?! "Marge, you crappin' in there? What're you doin'?"

Silence.

"Marge?"

"I'm okay," she called; it was obvious that she was crying. "I'll be out . . . in a second."

Norm Gellis swung his feet to the floor. He stood. He was naked. "What in the fuck are you *crying* about, Marge?"

"I've got a right."

"You've got a *what*?" He moved quickly to the bathroom doorway. Marge was sitting on the toilet—the cover was down—she was wearing her pink flannel pajama top, and a pair of white cotton underwear. Her legs were together, elbows on her knees, her face covered by her hands. Norm repeated, "You've got a *what*, Marge?"

She said nothing.

"Are you some kinda woman's libber, Marge?" He chuckled. "You gonna tell me why you're sittin' on the toilet there, cryin', while I'm standin' here in need of takin' a shit? Or am I gonna have to guess and go shit out the window?"

She said nothing. She continued weeping.

"Why don'tcha just get up offa there, Marge? Some of us got better things to do. It's a Saturday, you know, and these men around here are all gonna be home, and I got real important things to discuss with 'em." He waited a moment; Marge stayed where she was. "Hey, woman, I'm talking to you!"

She slowly took her hands away from her face; she looked up at him; her eyes were bloodshot, her face flushed and puffy from crying. She smiled a small, quivering smile. "Menopause," she said. "Hot flashes. That's all, Norm. Just hot flashes."

Norm chuckled again. "Yeah, well I got a hot flash for you, Marge—if you don't get up offa that toilet I'm gonna crap right in yer lap."

She stood. Head down, she moved past him and into the bedroom. "I'm sorry, Norm."

"Hey," he said, "women cry. I can't do nothin' about it, even if I wanted to."

Marge nodded slowly. She glanced at the window; the drapes were open, and the morning sunlight seemed much brighter than usual. She went to the window and looked out. She gasped.

Timmy Meade pushed his face briefly against his bedroom window. He stepped back and smiled.

The first snow of the year was on Granada—two

inches of white fluff on the roofs and shrubs and
on the thinnest branches of trees, snow that was
not yet corrupted by car exhausts, and by the dirt
that always hung, unseen, in the air.

He moved back to the window. He squinted, as
if that would help him to see better. Someone had
been walking in that first snow, already, he saw—
the tracks were everywhere, like a million wrinkles
on a huge white bedsheet. Somebody had been
walking around in it in their bare feet.

He scowled. Damn it! Why would they do that?
Why would they ruin it for him?

He stepped back from the window.

He thought a moment. He remembered.

Then, puzzled by what he had just seen and
disbelieving, he stepped back to the window and
looked once more.

The Harrises' bedroom contained two windows.
One faced west ("A very nice view," the real estate
agent had explained. "And so it will remain for
some time, because Mr. Reynolds doesn't plan to
build any new homes out there until some drainage problems have been solved"), and the other
window faced east; it overlooked the front porch
roof.

Shelly Harris, dressed in a red and black night-
gown, stood facing that window now, her eyes on
the porch roof.

She was on the verge of a scream. She was
seeing something she could not hope to understand.

Dick Wentis became aware that his mouth was
hanging open, and he thought dimly that he had
never imagined that that sort of thing ever hap-

pened—he had always assumed it was just a literary device.

"You've been standing there a long time," Trudy said. "Deep in thought?"

He glanced around at her. "Could you come over here, Trudy, and tell me if you see what I see?"

She smiled, confused: "What?"

"Just come here, please." He turned back to the window.

Trudy climbed out of the waterbed, threw a robe around herself, and walked over to him. She stood on her tiptoes and looked over his shoulder. "It snowed, huh?" she said.

Dick stepped to one side. "The footprints, Trudy. Look at the footprints."

She looked.

Lorraine Graham saw the footprints, and the new snow, and the frigid blue sky, and the cluster of houses around her.

She said, "Stan, it's really beautiful, really very nice."

She felt his arm around her waist; she smelled his aftershave; she heard him whisper something passionate, as he always did in the morning.

And she said, giggling a little, "But what about the boys, Stan?"

"To hell with the boys."

She thought about that a moment. "Yes," she said. "To hell with them." And she stepped very slowly away from the window, and the new snow, and the footprints.

Janice McIntyre turned from her window to face her husband, her eyes wide. "My God," she said, "they're *every*where! But that's not possible, is it? It's not possible!"

Miles was seated on the edge of the bed, elbows on his knees, hands clasped. "It's some kind of practical joke," he told her. "Somebody got hold of some ladders—"

"Those footprints are on the *roof* of the house across the street, Miles. And they're on the Wentises' roof, too—I can *see* them!"

"The carpenters have ladders tall enough, Jan. This *is* a construction site."

"Miles, the carpenters left a week ago."

He sighed, "Yes, I know."

"Then can you tell me what happened? Did someone drive in here while we were sleeping? Can you explain it, Miles?"

"No," he said immediately. "I can't explain it. Not right now, anyway. But I'm going to get my clothes on, and I'm going to go outside, and maybe *then* I'll be able to explain it. Okay?"

She stared silently at him a moment; then, "I'm scared, Miles," she said.

Chapter 25

Most of them were dressed in winter coats thrown over pajamas and nightgowns, and they gravitated, through the new snow, to the center of Granada (a half-acre size circle of open land which, said the brochure distributed to prospective home buyers, "will house a children's playground, decorative bandstand, and lush botanical gardens"), their eyes on the footprints all the while. Most stayed clear of them, as if stepping on them or in them would bring bad luck, or as if the footprints—strange as they were—were somehow inviolate.

Norm Gellis was there, and so was his wife, her face still red and puffy from crying, though the tears had long since stopped. Norm's gaze darted from one line of footprints to another, and he whispered "Jesus!" over and over again.

Timmy Meade and Sam Wentis—Timmy in pajamas and heavy winter coat, and Sam in jeans and a flannel shirt—stood quietly together. Dora and Larry Meade were nearby, also silent. Larry

felt an inner chill—a feeling he couldn't explain—
and it scared him.

Dick and Trudy Wentis stood with Janice McIn-
tyre. "Where's Miles?" Dick Wentis asked. And
Janice, nodding toward her house, answered,
"Checking for signs of a ladder."

"I've checked already," Dick said. "There are
none." And he fell silent.

Shelly and Malcolm Harris—their infant daughter Serena bundled up in Shelly's arms—wandered
over. After a long, clumsy moment of silence, Malcolm said, "This kind of thing happened once before,
you know." And he made a bad attempt at a smile.

"Did it?" said Dick Wentis, without enthusiasm.

"Yes. Late in the nineteenth century, I think. In
Pennsylvania."

"The Devil's Footprints," Janice cut in, at a whisper. And she found that all eyes were suddenly on
her. "Well," she hurried on, as if in apology, "that's
what they called them, anyway. Three-toed footprints, like a deer's, I imagine. Only larger. And
they were everywhere. Like these footprints are.
There was even some evidence that whoever—
whatever—made the footprints had walked up the
sides of houses."

Sound carried well in the chill, quiet morning
air, and Dora and Larry Meade, not far away,
heard what Janice was saying and came over.
Timmy Meade and Sam Wentis followed moments
later.

Janice looked from one face to another. Each face
was alive with anticipation. Finally, she said, shrug-
ging, "That's all I know. They were never able to
explain the footprints, I can tell you that."

Miles appeared. He was shaking his head slowly, in confusion. "Weirdest goddamned thing . . ." he muttered.

"What did you find?" Janice asked.

"I didn't find anything," he answered. "No ladder marks, anyway." He paused; then, "Has anyone called the sheriff?"

"We don't need him," Norm Gellis called. He was at the back of the small circle of people.

"I called him," Dick Wentis said.

Norm Gellis shouldered his way to the front of the circle. "We don't need the sheriff here," he said again. With agitation. "What good has he been to us, so far? No good at all—am I right or wrong?" He paused only a moment. "I'm right," he continued. "Because we've got two boys missing, we've got a damned bus crash, we've got kids breaking into our houses while we're asleep, it's happened to *me* twice!" He held up two fingers. "Twice," he repeated. "And now we've got this . . . this stupid, damned *prank*—"

"You're Mr. Gellis, aren't you?" Dick Wentis cut in, straining to sound cordial.

He nodded quickly, "Uh-huh," and stuck his hand out.

Dick took it; he let it go quickly. "Trudy told me what you had to say a couple weeks back, Mr. Gellis."

"Did she now?"

"The way she explains it, you're a bit of a hothead, aren't you?"

"Yeah, sometimes," he answered, grinning. "I admit it."

The response took Dick off guard; he was momentarily at a loss for a reply.

"Maybe we should listen to Mr. Gellis," Malcolm Harris suggested.

Dick said, "I don't think so."

And they all heard the wail of a police siren behind them.

Evening

"I'm scared again," said Janice McIntyre. She was in her big brown wicker chair; Miles stood behind their small bar at the opposite end of the room, drink in hand. (Janice, patting her now plainly swollen abdomen, had declined his offer of a scotch and soda, and settled for ginger ale instead.)

"Scared?" he said. "Why?"

"Are you going to tell me you aren't scared, Miles?"

"Of what, precisely? Kids' footprints in the snow?" He sipped his drink and pretended to chuckle.

"That's asinine, Miles."

He set his drink down and leaned forward, both hands on the edge of the bar. "Listen," he said, summoning up his most serious tone, "the sheriff was right; it was just a stupid, giant-sized, and very clever practical joke. Nothing more. How could it have *been* anything more than that, Janice? There really are no ghosts, you know."

She did not answer.

He went on, trying a different approach, "It's like watching a magic show. Things are never what they appear to be. If you see a magician tear a newspaper up, and then he throws it to the ground, and suddenly it's whole again—well then, you have to assume that it can't be the newspaper which was torn up, or that he never tore it up in the first place. Simple. Do you understand what I'm trying to tell you, Janice?"

She sighed. "Yes, Miles, I understand what you're trying to tell me, and I think you're rationalizing the whole thing. I think you're denying it merely because you can't explain it."

He sipped his drink again, then said pointedly, "For our own sanity, Janice, it's the only thing we can do."

She answered immediately, "No, it isn't, it most certainly isn't the only thing we can do." She stood abruptly. She left the room.

Miles listened, confused, as she went up the stairs. "Janice?" he called.

"It's for us," she called back. "For me and the baby. And for you, too—if you want."

Malcolm Harris reluctantly took the gun that Norm Gellis offered him. It was the Weatherby 20 gauge—an ugly damned thing, Malcolm thought. "I haven't held one of these in twenty years," he said nervously. Its long barrels gleamed darkly at him in the living room's fluorescent light. "I'm not even sure how to load it."

Norm leaned over and released a small catch near the trigger. "Okay," he said, "now crack it open."

Malcolm opened the weapon at the middle, exposing two chambers, one above the other. Norm handed him two shells. "It's lead shot, Malcolm. I had a devil of a time getting 'em—damned government's outlawed 'em practically everywhere—but they're a hell of a lot better than steel."

Malcolm fingered the shells uncertainly. "I don't know—maybe we should leave the whole thing to . . ." He faltered.

"Leave it to who, Malcolm? That damned idiot sheriff who doesn't know a bad situation when it comes up and bites him on the cock? Or maybe to the Penn Yann police? Shit, they can't even find two lost little boys. They'd probably get into trouble tryin' to find their own assholes, for Chrissakes! No, I'll tell you again, Malcolm—"

"Mal. Please. Just Mal."

"Mal—I'll tell you again. This is *our* fight, and *our* responsibility, and no one but us can see that it's taken care of properly." He nodded at Shelly, on the couch; she was holding Serena; Marge was sitting quietly beside her. "Tell me this, Mal—how much does that pretty wife and that beautiful baby mean to you? How much?"

"Everything, of course," Malcolm answered quickly.

"Then it's for *them* you gotta do this. Not for me or for yerself, really. But for them. Okay?"

Malcolm thought a moment. He put a shell in the bottom chamber of the Weatherby 20 gauge. "Okay," he said and loaded the top chamber. "But I'll tell you this, Norm—we didn't move here expecting to have to do this kind of thing."

Norm grinned. "Hey, Mal, what can I tell ya?! Read the newspapers—things are gettin' tough all over. The blacks are riotin', and the spicks are riotin', the cities are fallin' apart, people are killin' other people left and right. That's why I came out here. But now, the trouble's trying to catch up with me." He grinned. "But we're not gonna let it catch up, are we, Mal?"

Malcolm shook his head briskly, his resolve suddenly much firmer.

"Mal," Shelly called, "could you toss the diaper bag over." It was next to his chair. "Serena's soaked."

Malcolm reached for the bag. Norm touched his knee. "It's for her, Mal. Remember that," he whispered. "It's for her and for the little one."

Chapter 26

Sanity came back to Lorraine Graham like an unwanted guest. It gnawed at the edges of her illusions, it altered them, made them quiver.

Until at last, her dead husband grinned at her, and his mouth widened, and he became, very quickly, the Cheshire cat, and, like the Cheshire cat, he lost his parts one by one.

Then he laughed.

And Lorraine was overcome by the darkness. She murmured the names of her boys: "Robin? Robert?" Then she said aloud, "I know it's passé, Stan, and all the books are right about giving twins a chance to be individuals. But these are *only* names, after all."

Stan said nothing. Thirteen years ago, he had disagreed vehemently. Now he could say nothing.

Lorraine climbed out of the bed and scuffed across the floor to the light switch. She flicked it on.

She screamed Stan's name into the empty room

only once. Because, instead of summoning him again, the name merely echoed in her ears, and made them ring.

Like a hungry animal, the real world was upon her. And she knew that fighting it was useless. Stan had proved that. And Robin, and Robert, and her mother. So, she decided, she would become a part of it.

She would let it swallow her up.

Simple.

Miles McIntyre stood in his bedroom doorway and watched in dismay as Janice transferred clothes from her chest of drawers to two open suitcases on the bed. "I'm sorry, Janice," he said, "but I really have no concrete idea why you're doing this."

She stopped midway between the bed and the chest of drawers. She sighed. "No," she said, as if in apology. "Of course you don't—how could you?"

"Is it that you don't trust me, Jan?"

She shook her head quickly. "It's not a matter of trust, Miles. I trust you implicitly." She lowered her head, suddenly aware of the basic unfairness of what she was doing. "Tell me something," she went on, and looked him squarely in the eye. "How do you feel about ghosts?"

He grinned. "Are you serious?" The question was genuine.

She closed her eyes; she inhaled deeply. "I love you, Miles," she said on the exhale, "so I'll ask again . . ."

"What do you want me to think about them, Jan? I don't believe in them, I don't disbelieve in them."

"And if I told you there's a ghost in this house?"

He answered immediately, "I'd say that was very romantic. Every house should have one."

She said nothing. She moved stiffly, with sudden agitation, to the chest of drawers; she opened the third drawer, withdrew a half dozen maternity smocks.

After a long silence, Miles said incredulously, "You're fucking serious!"

She looked up at him from packing one of the suitcases. "You're damned right, Miles!"

"And that's why you're leaving?"

"Yes," she answered. "And because . . . of the footprints."

"Can we at least talk about it first?"

"You talk. I'll listen." She continued packing.

"Yes," Miles said tentatively. "Yes." But, in spite of his desperation, he could think of nothing else to say.

And Janice continued to pack.

Malcolm Harris's night vision had never been good, and now, under a blanket of clouds, and without even the faint luminescence of the morning's snow—it had melted almost completely before sunset—and with his back to the lights of Granada, he felt like a blind man.

He had asked himself the same question a half dozen times since coming here, to the perimeter of Granada (marked by a long, narrow ditch awaiting sewer pipe). What was he doing with a gun in his hands (he had always hated guns), and why had he taken up with a man who seemed to possess barely intelligence enough to speak, let alone to make hard and important decisions about their safety and security? But, he asked himself now,

was that really fair? Norm was uneducated, true,
and a little prejudiced—wasn't everyone?—but he
was by no means a stupid man. He seemed, in
fact, Malcolm decided, to have the tough, gut
instincts—the crude and inarticulate, but very basic,
common sense—that all men like him (who were
devoid of pretension, who dealt with life on its own
mean terms) seemed to have. And that, Malcolm
decided at last, was why he was here. With a gun
in his hands. He was facing life. He was doing,
after all, one of the things that he, as a man, was
designed to do. He was responding to a very real
danger. And if the others couldn't see that, then,
hell, they were the ones who were blind.

"Norm," he said, "I can't see a thing."

Norm Gellis, twenty yards west of him, chuckled
shortly. "Yeah, well they're there, believe me."

"I mean, I literally can't see a thing, Norm. It's
my night vision. It's always been loused up."

(The plan, as Norm had outlined it, was to "make
our presence known to them. That's very important, Malcolm. We just show 'em we're here, and
that we're prepared"—he patted his rifle—"and
we hope it's enough. If it ain't—well then, we
make other plans."

(It had seemed to make sense.

(And this place, halfway between Granada and
the woods, had seemed the best place to make
their stand. "I know they ain't comin' in by way of
the gate, Malcolm. They can't. So they gotta be
comin' in by way of the woods.")

"You shoulda told me about your goddamned
night vision before," Norm called. "What was I
supposed to do?—read your mind?"

"I guess I just didn't think about it, Norm. I'm sorry."

"Jesus H. How do you know it won't get better if you just stay out here for a while?"

"Norm, it's a problem I've had practically all my life."

"Shit! Okay. Let's work it this way. Let's just stay put and see what happens. *I* can see, anyway. And so can they. And that's all that really matters."

"How long, Norm?"

"Long as it takes. All night, maybe. Whatsa matter, you cold now? You wanta go home for a blanket?"

"No." Malcolm tried to ignore Norm's sarcasm. "It's okay. You're right—all night, if necessary. It's just that I was going to go into the office a little early tomorrow—"

"You wanta be quiet, Malcolm, or can'tcha hear, either?—'cuz *they* sure can."

Malcolm fell silent. Maybe, he thought, this one night would be enough.

"Robin?" Lorraine Graham said. "Robert? Stan? Mom?" She put her hand on the vertical posts of Granada's main gate. She repeated the names of her sons, her husband, her mother—a litany of ghosts, an empty and dreary account of what her life had once been, but could never be again.

She had toyed with the idea of starting over, of finding a man, and marrying him, and having sons. But it would take too much effort, she decided. And too much time. And she was too old, of course, and too tired. And nobody ever really starts over, do they? They go on to something else, something different. Which was something she simply did not want to do.

Granada's gate was colder than the air. She took her hands from it. She turned. She walked back through Granada, her steady gaze on the squat, dark line of woods in front of her:

It looked like a mouth. Closed. That would open for her.

Malcolm Harris tried in vain to focus on the pale, elongated figure moving very slowly and very gracefully in the blackness about fifty yards north of where he stood.

"Norm?" he said, his voice low.

Silence.

He mentally visualized the lay of the land around him. To the south, a long line of dense thickets stretched from the road to the woods. To the west, the land was clear for several hundred yards. To the east, Granada. And to the north, a dozen acres of untended apple trees. And there was also a path, he realized. Rundown, and unused, but, long ago, men had probably driven tractors on it, and hauled haywagons over it.

The elongated, whitish figure was walking on that path, he knew. "Norm?!" he called again, louder.

"You say something?" he heard. He turned his head; he saw Norm's short, squat shape as only a dark swell in the blackness. "Norm, there's someone over there."

"Over where?" Eagerly.

"North of us. On that path."

Norm rushed over to him. "Where?"

Malcolm turned his head back. He nodded. He said nothing. The figure was gone.

"*Where?*" Norm insisted.

"But she *was* there, Norm. She really was!" She? he wondered. Why had he said 'she'?

"I thought you couldn't see in the dark, Malcolm."

"I can see some things."

"Yeah, and that's just what yer doin' now—"

"Jesus," Malcolm cut in, "this is getting damned stupid!"

Then, from somewhere in the darkness, they heard, "Norm, there's someone over there!"

"My God!" Malcolm whispered, "That was *my* voice!"

Norm slowly brought his rifle up to a firing position.

"Jesus Christ!" Malcolm screeched. "What in the hell are you doing?" And he grabbed for the barrel of the rifle.

Norm yanked it away. "Little bastards!" he hissed.

And, like glass breaking, sudden, brittle laughter erupted all around them.

"My God!" Malcolm said again.

Norm fired. Once. Then again.

The laughter stopped.

And that is when they saw the fire.

Miles McIntyre was talking about investments and interest payments and equities, and Janice, as he talked, was growing angrier by the moment.

"So you see, darling," Miles concluded, "if we sell this house now we'll probably end up in the red, and the real question is—Where are we going to move to? That's the real question, Jan. Because new housing, these days, is getting awfully hard to find. Mr. Reynolds had a hell of a time getting an okay for this project—you know that, don't you? And if you're going to say, 'Well, let's get an older home,' I'll have to tell you that—"

Janice's interruption was pitched just slightly above a whisper, but it was tight and urgent, and it made Miles stop talking in midsentence: "My parents will welcome me in a second, Miles!" And she closed the suitcase hard and walked over to the phone on the nightstand near the bed. She put her hand on the receiver. "It's up to you, Miles."

He said nothing for a long moment, his mind darting from one possibility to another. "Yes," he said finally. "We'll sell the house. I'll call Mr. Jenner in the morning. I think we can get a buyer in about a month—"

"That's not good enough, Miles." She picked up the receiver, began to dial.

He rushed over, grabbed the receiver from her, put it back on the cradle. "A compromise, Jan," he pleaded. "Two weeks. That's all I want. It's what I'll tell Jenner. And if there's no buyer by then, okay—we'll go to your parents', or to a motel—"

"You think I'll change my mind, don't you, Miles?"

"Yes," he admitted. "But if you don't, I promise you we *will* leave. Okay?"

She moved silently to the closed suitcase, opened it, withdrew the maternity smocks. She looked over at him. "Miles," she said, "I do love you, you must know that. Otherwise—" And she carried the maternity smocks to her chest of drawers and put them away. Her gaze settled on the window. She wondered what was causing the wildly shifting red glow on the closed drapes.

*   *   *

The fire had been building for some time; now
Malcolm watched, awestruck, as it played hotly
and brightly inside the house; for the moment it
was contained by windows, and doors, and insulation. After another few minutes, the windows would
implode from the heat and partial vacuum behind
them, and the flames would erupt crazily into the
chill evening air.

Norm stared blankly at the fire.

Malcolm dropped the Weatherby 20 gauge. He
wanted desperately to know the time. Because, if
he and Norm hadn't returned by ten o'clock, Shelly
and Serena were going to go back home. And if it
was past ten, then that's where they were, now. At
home. And if they were at home, they were dead.

Because it was his house that was burning so
fiercely.

Part Five

THE STORM

From *The Penn Yann Post Gazette*, December 6:

FIRE DESTROYS GRANADA HOME

Fire last night leveled a home at 22 Morningside Way, Granada. The fire, which, according to fire investigators, started in the kitchen of the big, eight-room luxury home, was discovered only after it had apparently gutted the interior of the house.

The home belonged to Malcolm and Shelly Harris, who were visiting friends in Granada when the fire began. The only person hurt in the fire was volunteer fireman Coby Pinkins, Jr., who was treated for minor burns and smoke inhalation, at Myers Community Hospital, and released.

According to investigators, arson has not been totally ruled out as a possible cause . . .

Chapter 27

December 10

"You know," Sam Wentis said, "if you squint"—he squinted severely, as if to demonstrate—"it looks like nothin' happened, like you could walk right in and sit down and have your supper. Don'tcha think it looks like that?" He looked questioningly at Timmy Meade. "I mean, if you squint?"

"Yeah," Timmy Meade answered. "I guess." He squinted briefly. "Yeah. 'Cept for 'round the windows"—where the flames had blackened the yellow vinyl siding and twisted it into grotesque shapes. "Anyway, they're gonna bulldoze it. That'll be fun to watch. I guess they're 'gonna do it next week."

Sam Wentis said nothing.

"Don't you think it'll be fun to watch, Sam?"

"What if they kept right on goin'," Sam Wentis said, and he turned his head slowly so his gaze swept over all of Granada.

"Why would they wanta do that, Sam?"

He said nothing.

"Sam?"

"Where you wanta go to, Timmy? You wanta go into the woods? You wanta go over to Riley's Glen?"

It was a cold, clear morning. A Sunday. And Granada seemed very quiet and empty. From far to his right, Timmy heard the Gellises' new dog begin barking rhythmically (the dog seemed to bark, he thought, for no reason at all, which was okay, because it was kind of a lazy, soothing bark, especially from far away, and it was good to have a dog in Granada).

"It's a shit damn German Shepherd!" Sam Wentis said, nodding in the direction of the barking dog. "A shit damn killer!"

"Naw," said Timmy Meade, grinning. "There's this cat runs loose—great big thing—and I seen it chase that dog right up on his back porch. Funniest shit damn thing I ever saw."

"Yeah, well my father says he's a shit damn killer!" Sam Wentis seemed offended. "My father says that and my father oughta know."

"You're right," Timmy said immediately. "You're dead right, Sam."

Sam looked suspiciously at him a moment. "So where you wanta go to?" he said again. "Riley's Glen? You wanta go there?"

"Sure," Timmy answered.

"That damned dog's barking again," Larry Meade said, looking out his kitchen window. "I thought we moved here to get away from that kind of thing."

"Is that why we moved here?" Dora said. She was seated at the kitchen table, hands around a cup of black coffee. "To get away from barking dogs?"

He glanced at her. "It was one of the reasons, anyway."

"To live 'the carefree country life'?" she continued expansively, sarcastically. " 'Fresh air and sunshine and good neighbors'?"

Larry said nothing. Their relationship—never a match made in heaven—had taken a nose dive in the last few weeks and he wasn't at all certain what direction he wanted this present discussion to take.

"Is that what the brochure told us, Larry?—'Fresh air and sunshine and good neighbors'?"

"I didn't read the brochure, Dora."

"Well I did. And it didn't say a thing about arsonists–"

"C'mon, Dora–"

"Or kidnappers, or the devil's fucking footprints–"

"Christ almighty!"

"I*t* said, 'Fresh air and sunshine and good neighbors,' or words very much to that effect. Jesus, what a crock *that* was! Over here"—she inclined her head toward the Harrises' burnt-out home—"we've got a remnant of the South Bronx. And over there"—she nodded toward the Gellis home—"we've got Mr. Exhibitionist, Gun Nut, and up over there" —she nodded to the east—"we've got the infamous Reynolds Road, barely wide enough for one car to pass over, and right here"—she thumped her chest with her fist—"we've got the world's A-Number-One sucker. Mrs. Sucker, that's me–"

"You sound a little angry," Larry cut in; he grinned at her. "Maybe even hysterical."

She grinned back at him. "You'd like that,

wouldn't you?! You'd like to watch cool Dora blow her stack. Well, *that* you won't see, my darling husband. They can burn this place down around me and you will *not* see me lose my cool!"

"Let's hope it doesn't come to that, because I know you're cool, Dora—fifty degrees below cool, as a matter of fact . . ."

"Go to hell!"

He raised an eyebrow and tried to think of a snappy reply. He could think of nothing. He turned back to the window; he saw that the Gellises' dog was still barking—louder, now, and at a faster tempo, as if something was agitating it. "To hell, indeed," Larry muttered.

"They were friends," Trudy Wentis explained. "Close friends. And now that Shelly's moved away, Lorraine's got no one. That's why I'm going over there."

Dick Wentis sighed. She was right, of course. "Just assure me, darling, that you're not planning to . . . endear yourself to her. I mean, nobody's seen her since the fire. It's obvious she just wants to be left alone."

Trudy straightened the collar of her brown wool coat and looked confusedly at him. "I'm surprised at you, Dick. What if I *did* endear myself to her— what's the harm in that?"

He shrugged. "No harm, really. I suppose it would be very humanitarian. It's just that I don't care very much for the idea of an emotionally disturbed woman dropping over unannounced and weeping all over us." He grimaced. "Jesus," he continued, his tone apologetic, "that sounded callous as hell, didn't it?!"

"Yes, Dick. It did." She opened the front door. "I won't be long. And don't worry—I won't bring her back with me."

She rang the Grahams' doorbell again. For the fifth time. Because, there was no doubt, someone was in the house. The closed curtains on the picture window had parted very slightly after the second ring. And besides, the house *felt* as if someone were in it—the same feeling, Trudy thought, that she got whenever she called someone on the telephone and *knew* whether or not there would be an answer. In the same way, she now knew that someone was in the Graham house. It was intuition, and it was never wrong.

She stepped back from the door and scanned the front of the house. She cupped her hands around her mouth: "Lorraine?" she called. She waited a few moments and got no response. "Are you all right, Lorraine?" Still nothing.

"Maybe she just wants to be left alone," Dick said from behind her.

She jumped a little and turned quickly to face him. "Jesus Christ, Dick! Why don't you announce yourself?!"

He nodded at the Graham house. "Like I told you, she's either not home or she just wants to be left alone. Why don't you wait till tomorrow?"

"She might be in trouble, Dick." *Intuition?* she wondered. "She might have . . . done something to herself."

"Of course she's in trouble, Trudy. She's lost both of her sons, for God's sake. How would you feel?"

"But I saw the curtains move, Dick." She nodded at the picture window. "*Some*one is in there."

"Which proves she just wants to be left alone, Trudy. If she's got strength enough to peek out the window, she's got strength enough to open the door. Now why don't you come away from there and we'll try again later."

"We?"

"Both of us. And if there's still no answer . . . I don't know, I'll pick the lock or something. Okay?" He took her hand and coaxed her away from the house.

"Okay," she said. "But remember—you promised . . ."

Marge Gellis said to her husband, "The neighbors are going to get angry, Norm." She lowered her head. "No," she continued hurriedly. "I'm sorry." And she wandered back into the kitchen.

"You mean because of the dog?" Norm called. "He's like the guns, Marge, you know that. He's protection." Norm got out of his living room chair and joined his wife in the kitchen. "And besides, Marge, these damn houses are soundproof—almost, anyway. And Joe don't bark *that* much."

"Yes," Marge said quietly; she slowly poured some pancake batter into a frying pan. "Yes, I know."

Norm nodded at the stove. "You'd better turn the burner on, Marge, or that pancake's gonna take a hell of a long time to cook." He pretended to chuckle.

She turned the burner on.

"Marge?"

"Yes?"

"You got some kinda problem, Marge?"

"No."

" 'Cuz you been like a damn spook, lately. What's it—that menopause thing again?"

She said nothing.

"Or are you still mad about what me and Malcolm Harris tried to do?" He paused briefly. "Maybe you think it was *my* fault his house burnt down."

"No," she said quietly.

Norm stared at her a moment. "Marge," he said, his tone soft, his words measured and slow, "things . . . are getting kinda shitty, aren't they?!"

She flipped the pancake; she said nothing.

"I admit it, Marge. And maybe some of it's my fault." He waited. She ladled the pancake onto a plate. "I just wantcha to know something, Marge." She poured more pancake batter into the frying pan. "I wantcha to know"—he looked away—"that what I'm doin'—it's all for you, Marge." He waited again, felt a nervous smile playing on his lips. " 'Cuz I love ya, Marge."

She tried to get the spatula under the just-poured pancake batter. The pancake hadn't yet cooked enough. "Damn it to hell!" she whispered.

Norm left the room. He cursed himself; he felt very foolish.

Chapter 28

The Riley's Glen Campsites—which lay a half mile outside the southeast perimeter of Granada—consisted of a dozen park benches, a half dozen concrete and stone fireplaces (in various stages of repair), and a small green plaque, imbedded in a square of granite, commemorating "The spot where, in 1733, Nathan Riley established the first Community Smokehouse in the region of Penn Yann."

Sam Wentis kicked idly at the plaque. "What's a smokehouse?" he asked.

Timmy Meade answered immediately, and with great authority, "It's where people go to smoke."

"Yer fulla shit," Sam Wentis said.

"No I'm not."

"Yes you are, 'cuz a smokehouse ain't where people go to smoke."

"Yeah?" said Timmy Meade. "What is it, then?"

"I don't know—but it *ain't* where people go to smoke."

Timmy Meade decided not to press the subject.

*   *   *

The snowfall began lazily. A few large flakes settled onto the brown, autumn leaves that covered the ground here to several inches, and Timmy Meade watched sadly as the flakes quickly melted. "It's too damned warm," he murmured.

"Too damned warm," Sam Wentis said.

They had not been watching the sky. The walk to Riley's Glen from Granada was through small stands of woods and underbrush, and it was a dangerous walk unless you kept your eyes on the ground. So they hadn't seen the quickly advancing line of dark gray clouds coming at them from the north.

Timmy Meade saw it now. "Jesus damn!" he said. "We'd better head home!"

And Sam Wentis said, "Head home!"

The ragged front edge of the storm was almost directly overhead, and the wind had strengthened noticeably, pulling frigid Arctic air in with it. Timmy Meade shivered, more in anticipation of what was coming than the cold or the wind itself. Because he could see what was coming—and, he realized, it was sweeping into Granada at that very moment. ("Like a crazy old woman with a giant whisk broom," he remembered his father telling him years before, about a similar storm.)

"Head home!" Sam Wentis said again.

And then, as if it had been straining angrily at some vast, invisible barrier, and had finally broken through it, the storm was upon them.

Timmy Meade found that he couldn't speak, that the sudden and incredibly strong wind wouldn't let him. And, like a thousand tiny bees, the hard, furious snowfall stung his eyes and eyelids, and the exposed skin of his face and neck. He turned his back to the wind; he put his head down and closed his eyes; he hugged himself tightly for warmth. "Sam!" he screamed, and he barely heard himself above the awful frenzy of the storm. "We gotta . . . hide somewhere."

He waited a full minute.

He heard nothing from Sam Wentis.

"We've got all hell coming at us now," said Larry Meade. "Jesus, they didn't say anything about this over the radio." He let go of the curtain on the big picture window, turned and faced Dora; she was in a Queen Anne chair on the other side of the large room. "Let's make sure everything's closed up tight, Dora. I have a feeling this storm isn't going to give up right away."

She pushed herself out of the chair reluctantly. "We've got to talk, Larry."

He looked quizzically at her a moment, then understood. "We'll talk later."

"Larry, I am *sick* of this whole charade."

"That's very theatrical, Dora, but let's check out the house first, okay?"

"And I'm sick of you, too—"

He cut in urgently, "Dora, where's Timmy?"

"He's with the Wentis kid. I told them not to go far from the house. Now are we going to talk or not?"

"Then why aren't they *here*, Dora?"

"Christ, I don't know. They probably went to the Wentises'."

Larry rushed to the phone; he hurriedly dialed the Wentises' number.

"Dick? This is Larry Meade. Is my son there?"

"Timmy? No. I was just going to call you, in fact–"

"Hold on, Dick." He glanced at Dora. "What was Timmy wearing, Dora?"

"I don't know," she began, trying to remember. "His denim jacket, I suppose–"

"Christ almighty! You sent him out there dressed in his denim jacket?!"

"It was warmer this morning, Larry. I didn't know we were going to get a damned blizzard. What are you getting so excited about?"

"You seem to forget, Dora, that two other little boys have turned up missing."

Dora said nothing.

Larry said to Dick, "I'll be over in a minute. We've got to go looking for them."

Norm Gellis groped blindly for the latch on Joe's collar while Joe whimpered pathetically at him. "It's okay, dog," Norm said. "We'll get you inside and put you down in the cellar and you'll be warm as toast. What'd you think—I was gonna leave you out here to freeze your poor nuts off?" Norm wished frantically that he'd put his gloves on. The task of finding the small latch on Joe's metal collar—a task made difficult, anyway, by the storm, and by Joe's nervous twitching—was made almost impossible by the fact that his fingers had become numb already, and so were next to useless. "Fucking shit!" Norm hissed. Finally, he found the latch; he twisted it hard to the left; it wouldn't give. "Goddamnit!"

Joe whimpered louder.

"Shut up!" Norm commanded, and whacked the

dog on the snout with his open left hand. The dog stopped whimpering abruptly.

"Fucking damned dog!"

He twisted the latch again. It was frozen. "Chrissakes!"

He took the tether in one hand and followed it to where it was attached to a post screwed into the ground twenty feet away. He put his hands on the post and winced at the burning coldness of the metal; he turned the post counterclockwise, aware—as it gave with agonizing slowness in the hardened soil—that the wind and cold were sapping his strength by the second. He thought about going back into the house for a breather, and to put his gloves on, when he realized that Joe's tether had slackened. "Joe?" he said. He pulled the tether; it was broken. In panic, Norm realized Joe had broken it.

"Goddamned fucking dog!" he screeched. "Goddamnit it all to hell fucking dog you're going to freeze your fucking nuts off!"

He stood silently beside the post and broken tether for several minutes, wondering what, precisely, he was going to do.

"Mr. Jenner?" Janice McIntyre realized she was whispering into the receiver and that the man on the other end of the line probably couldn't hear her. She put her hand over the mouthpiece and cleared her throat. She took her hand from the mouthpiece. "Mr. Jenner?" she said again, louder.

"Yes, this is Jenner."

"Is my husband there, Mr. Jenner? This is Janice McIntyre. Miles had an appointment with you."

"Yes, Mrs. McIntyre, your husband arrived not

more than two minutes ago. Would you like to speak with him?"

"Yes, thank you."

A short pause, then Miles came on the line. "Janice? What's wrong?"

"I was worried, Miles. About you, I mean, and this storm—"

Miles exhaled, as if pretending to be out of breath. "I barely outran it. I don't think it'll last long, though. These things usually blow themselves out pretty quickly."

"You're not going to try and drive back through it, are you?"

"On Reynolds Road? It'd be suicide. No, believe me, I'm going to wait until I hear the all clear signal."

"I'm glad to hear that, Miles." She smiled. "And you're right; it shouldn't last long."

"Of course I'm right, Jan. Now I've got to get back to Jenner—you *do* still want to sell the house, don't you?"

"Yes, of course—"

"It was a rhetorical question, Jan. I'll be home when I can, but don't hold supper for me. Bye." He hung up.

Janice hung up.

Her smile faded. She had always liked storms— summer storms, winter storms; they were so beautifully chaotic, so humbling, and they provided a wonderful time for reflection.

But this storm—so big, and so loud, and so sudden—was like a quick slap in the face, a screamed obscenity. It should really have announced itself first, she thought.

*   *   *

With effort, Larry Meade pushed the door closed behind him. Dick Wentis was waiting; he had dressed well for the storm—a long goose-down-filled coat, Timberland boots, heavy, oversized wool mittens. He flipped the hood on his coat up and nodded to indicate the suede gloves Larry was wearing. "Your hands will freeze in five minutes, Larry." He looked toward the stairway. "Trudy," he called, "would you bring down my other pair of mittens, please."

"Thanks," Larry said.

Trudy called, from upstairs, "Where are they?"

"Fourth drawer down," Dick answered, and turned again to Larry. "The boys could be any of a number of places, Larry. Did your son say anything to you?"

"No. We told them to stay close to the house." He shrugged. "Of course, you can't really *tell* the kid to do something. . . ."

Trudy appeared with the wool mittens; she handed them to Larry, he took them, peeled his suede gloves off quickly—as if embarrassed by them—and put the mittens on. He nodded to the west. "The boys liked to play in the woods. That's probably where they are now."

"That would be best," Dick said.

Larry looked questioningly at him.

"It's well protected from the wind," Dick explained. "But of course," he went on, "a lot of those trees are pretty old, and that wind is awfully strong . . ." He stopped, leaned over, kissed Trudy. "We won't be long," he said.

"I *can* come with you," she said, making it obvious that it had been a topic of prior discussion.

Larry patted her hand paternally. "I know you

can, and if we don't find them right away, I promise you—we'll bundle you up good . . ." He turned,
opened the front door slightly; he kissed her again.
"If you're worried," he said, "don't be."

Together, he and Larry left the house.

Chapter 29

Norm Gellis explained that Joe was missing, that he'd probably run off, "dumb ass dog that he is." Marge listened quietly, nodded in the right places, and when Norm was finished she went to the closet, got her best coat—gray wool, with a rabbit's fur collar—shrugged into it, and said, "I'm going to Mass now. Can I have the car keys?"

After a moment's confused hesitation, Norm said, "Are you out of your mind?"

"It's Sunday," she said, smiling pleasantly. "And Mass starts"—she checked her watch—"in an hour. It'll take me at least that long to–"

"You've gone fucking bananas!" Norm cut in; he found that the words made him grin, despite himself.

She stared blankly at him, as if unable to understand what he was saying. "Are they in your coat pocket?" she said at last.

"What?—my keys? Christ, Marge, it's a damned blizzard out there! And besides, you haven't been to Mass in years. The last time was the day after our honeymoon."

She stared blankly at him again. Finally, she removed her coat and hung it back up neatly. She started for the stairs. "I'm going to lie down a while, Norm. Call me when you want your lunch."

He watched her move very slowly and stiffly up the stairs. When she was on the landing, he whispered, "Marge, are you okay?" But she didn't hear him. She turned right, toward their bedroom. Norm thought fleetingly that she looked very old.

They huddled in a circle for warmth, their bodies touching, heads down, eyes closed.

The storm at the tops of the evergreens tossed pine needles and small twigs at them, and stiff, whirling undercurrents of the wind played madly with their long dark hair, and drove dead leaves around them, and into the circle.

Occasionally, one of the creatures imitated a bird's song, or a speech it had heard very recently. And another recreated, in miniature, the various noises of the storm. Still another laughed (the laughter of adults—deep, and tentative, and shrill, and postured—the quick, spontaneous laughter of children, the cooing and bubbly laughter of infants).

But mostly, there was silence. And a trembling, uncertain fear. Not the fear of death, but the fear of pain, which is a greater fear.

There were twenty of them. As one, they stood. And their heads turned in unison to the east, as if their gaze were on the small cluster of houses invisible through the woods and the storm.

Warmth was there.

In those houses.

Fifteen Years Earlier

Paul Griffin swung his feet to the floor, stood, grabbed the doorknob tightly, yanked his hand back. He cursed.

Rachel scrambled out of bed.

"The doorknob's hot!" Paul's voice was trembling. "It's the house, Rachel! It's on fire!"

"No," Rachel said steadily. "No. It can't be."

And they both saw the band of flickering yellow light beneath the door.

Paul ran to the window, opened its lock, pushed up. The window refused to move.

He glanced around. "Rachel," he ordered, "the washbasin! On the dresser! Quick, give it to me!"

Rachel grabbed the washbasin. "I don't understand, Paul. I don't understand," she said as she crossed the room. "We put the fire out. Why do you want this?" She gave him the washbasin. "I don't understand. Please, Paul . . ." She turned. "I don't understand." She crossed to the door. She put her hand on the doorknob. "Why don't we just—"

"Rachel, no!" Paul shouted.

She let go of the doorknob. She stepped back. Her body shook.

"Don't open that door, Rachel!"

"Yes," she murmured, "yes. I'm sorry."

Paul brought his arm back, washbasin in hand.

Rachel turned, faced him. "They did this, Paul. They want us to stay."

Paul brought his arm forward. "No," he whispered. He stopped the movement of his arm halfway to the window. "No!" he screamed. "No, you won't, you can't. I won't let you, she's not yours!"

He crossed the room.

He threw the door open.

Chapter 30

Larry Meade's small talk—managed here (in the open area between Granada and the stand of woods) at a level approximating a shout—was beginning to annoy Dick Wentis. He knew that the small talk was only Larry's way of denying what, exactly, they were doing—of dismissing it as just a passing unpleasantness that would soon be ended. Because Timmy and Sam had, after all, been missing for only half an hour at most, and by lunchtime everyone would probably be safe and snug at home.

"So," Larry shouted, "that's the scuttlebutt." He'd been talking about a minor sex scandal at his office. "She's going to be canned. I'm sure of it," he concluded, and felt suddenly foolish and insensitive—he wasn't sure why.

Visibility was at zero. The storm had intensified since sweeping into Granada, and Larry and Dick had found that in order to protect their eyes it was necessary to walk diagonally against the north wind, with their heads lowered at an uncomfortable angle.

("We should be able to relax a little once we get into the woods," Dick had explained shortly after leaving the house. "It's a natural sanctuary from the storm.")

Dick nodded to indicate an area just ahead of them. "Let's be careful," he shouted. "There's a ditch here, somewhere."

"A ditch?" Larry shouted. He turned his head slightly to look at Dick. "What kind of ditch?"

"For sewer pipe," Dick shouted back.

"Oh." Larry lifted his head and massaged his neck.

Then, for only a moment, the storm backed off slightly.

He opened his eyes wide. Abruptly, he stopped walking.

"Larry?" Dick said. He saw the man's lips move, saw the overwhelming fear and confusion that abruptly had settled over him; he heard nothing above the frenzy of the storm.

He put his arm over Larry's shoulders and forced him to a kneeling position—head lowered, his back and head protecting Larry from the storm and providing a relatively quiet air space to talk in: "Larry, what's wrong?" He found that he still had to raise his voice.

Larry's unfocused gaze was on the ground in front of his feet. The fear had left him; the confusion remained. He turned his head very slowly to look at Dick. He said, "Who are they, Dick?"

"I can't hear you, Larry. Talk louder!"

"I said, 'Who are they?' Those children." He nodded toward the woods. "There. Those children."

Dick looked where Larry had nodded. He saw

nothing. "What children, Larry? Timmy and Sam? Did you see Timmy and Sam?"

Larry looked up; he was smiling oddly. "Timmy and Sam aren't in the woods, Dick."

Dick said immediately, suddenly angered, "You can't know that! How can you know that?!"

"And even if they are . . . *even if they are*, Dick—we'll never find them!"

Dick felt the sudden anger building. He fought it back. Christ, this man was a fool! He grabbed Larry's arm and pulled him to a standing position. He pointed stiffly toward the woods; he shouted, "*That's* where *I'm* going, Larry! And you're coming with me if I have to kick your ass all the way there!"

The words WEATHER BULLETIN appeared at the bottom of the TV screen. Trudy Wentis turned the volume up.

"We were taken by surprise," the weatherman said. "The computer told us"—he grinned as if embarrassed—"that this low front"—he waved his wooden pointer at an area on a map of New York State which stretched diagonally west to east from the Pennsylvania border to Buffalo; a big "L" had been placed in the middle of the area—"was going to track much farther east and north of us, following this retreating band of high pressure"—he moved the pointer to indicate Lake Ontario and lower Canada. "However, this high pressure cell did not behave as our computer anticipated it would. It stalled here, around the Toronto area, and so the low pressure cell was deflected"—he moved the pointer—"into our region. Complicating it, and producing the very heavy snowfall and strong winds we are experiencing now, is another center of high pressure"—the map changed suddenly to a map of the entire eastern seaboard—"which is pulling moist air in from the Carolinas. This high pressure cell appears to be tracking to the east, however . . ."

Trudy turned the set off and mentally cursed weather forecasters, and computers, and high and low pressure cells. She crossed to the front window, parted the curtains with her hand; she saw nothing but a wall of wind-driven snow. She let go of the curtain.

She was getting nervous, she realized. It had been a full hour since Dick and Larry had left the house, and she thought the idea of bundling up tight and going out to look for them was becoming more and more appealing.

And there was the other thing, too—her intuition. As if it were a place inside her, a physical thing, she thought that something had settled into it, something small and prickly and alive—something that was whispering to her that all was not right in Granada. That something indeed was very, very wrong.

Janice McIntyre thought idly that it seemed almost like something Dr. Spock would have advised against—moving a baby's things to another house before the baby was born (bad for the emotional development of the fetus, maybe—interrupts the bonding procedure). She smiled wistfully, her gaze flitting from the print of Picasso's *Child with Dove*, to the fine Simmons crib, and the four-drawer chest, to the Welch basinette (only the best for little Melissa, or little Francis, or whoever it turned out to be), the tall, yellow changing table awaiting stacks of neatly folded diapers. It would all have to be repacked and set up in some other house, and that was a genuine shame because babies' rooms should always remain babies' rooms.

She flicked the light off. She put her hand on the doorknob and began to close the door. She felt something brush past her, as if a hand had touched her knees and thighs and her swollen abdomen very lightly.

She flicked the light on. She scanned the room. She saw nothing unusual. Only the light and shadow of the room. She decided there was a draft creeping into the house. From the storm. And she closed the door and went back downstairs.

Timmy Meade thought that building a quick, makeshift shelter out of the park tables and benches was just about the smartest thing anybody could have done. Because he was protected from the snow and the shit damn wind, and it wasn't so cold in here that he had to worry too much (although he wouldn't holler if it warmed up just a little). It was almost cozy, maybe a couple squirrels and chipmunks and such, caught out in the storm, would see what he'd done and decide to join him. That'd be all right. Hell, there was enough room for Sam Wentis, too. 'Course, he was probably at home by now, sitting down to a lunch of tomato soup and tuna fish sandwiches and a handful of Frito's corn chips.

And then, afterwards, a nap. Because he'd be tired, naturally, from tromping through the snow and the wind. And the cold always made people tired, too. But just a short nap, fifteen minutes or a half hour, 'cuz there was that shit damn homework

244 T. M. WRIGHT

to do for Mr. Armstrong (nobody else gave homework assignments, why should he?), and then a
good movie on TV . . .

He noticed, for the first time, that he was
shivering. Not quietly—the kind of shivering that
raised goosebumps—but violently, even noisily,
because he could see that his knees were knocking,
and that his jaw was quivering so much that his
teeth hit each other occasionally.

He found, also, that he could watch his knees
knocking and feel his jaw quivering as if he were
someone else, another boy watching from close by.

And that other boy laughed, because this dumb
kid huddled up inside a little house made of park
tables and park benches and shivering and shaking
like he was having some kind of a fit was just
about the funniest shit damn thing he ever saw.

Chapter 31

Norm Gellis called, "You asleep up there?" and waited just long enough to take a breath. "I said, 'Are you asleep up there?' Marge." He got no answer. "Damned spook. Mass, for Chrissakes, Mass!"

He went into the kitchen, opened the refrigerator door. "Shit!" What the world needed, he thought, what it really needed, was a refrigerator that automatically got rid of leftover macaroni, and the little molded jellos with dollops of whipped cream on top. A refrigerator that would disintegrate them, that would turn them into gray mush. *That's* what the world needed.

He slammed the refrigerator door. He listened. He wished the house wasn't quite so airtight and quite so soundproof. Because he knew the god-damned biggest storm of the decade was wailing away outside. But here, inside his new house, he could hear nothing.

Only dead silence.

And he hated silence.

Dear Norm,
  I feel like a girl again on my way to meet
some date my sister has fixed me up with. I
never knew the boys she fixed me up with till
we met, and it was always a surprise. That's
the way I feel, now, and it almost makes up
for what I'm doing.
  I wish I could say why, exactly, I am doing
this but I can't. Exactly.

Marge slowly reread what she'd written, then
wadded the paper into a tight ball and stuck it
into the pocket of her housedress. She'd have to
try again, because Norm wouldn't understand, and
it was imperative that he understand.

Trudy Wentis decided it was time. That she was
done fooling herself, done rationalizing. (*Well, Dick
and Larry and Sam and Timmy have found a safe,
secure, warm spot somewhere and they're waiting
there till the storm ends.*)
  She looked up the telephone number (taking
more time with it, she noted, than was necessary;
a way of putting off the inevitable, she realized),
dialed the number, began growing impatient by
the fifth ring, and by the twelfth ring her patience
had grown very thin indeed. Finally;
  "Sheriff's Department—Complaints; Officer Tibbe
speaking."
  Trudy exhaled. "Officer Tibbe, my name is Trudy
Wentis, I'm calling from Granada. Do you know
where that is?"
  "Yes, I do, Miss, Mrs . . ."

"*Mrs.* Wentis."

"Mrs. Wentis. I know where it is."

"I'm calling in regard to . . ." She paused, took a deep breath; this was a lot harder than she had thought it would be. "In regard to my son and my husband."

"Yes?"

She began nervously twirling the telephone cord around the forefinger of her right hand. "They're missing, Officer Tibbe. My husband and a friend of his went looking for my son—his name is Sam—about two hours ago, two and a half hours really, and they haven't come back yet. I'm just a little concerned, you understand . . ." She faltered.

"How long has your son been missing, Mrs. Wentis?"

"Sam? Since early this morning, since about 8:30 or 9:00, I guess. He was playing with a friend of his . . ."

"And I assume your husband went looking for him when the storm began?"

"Yes, that's right. He went with a neighbor of ours, Larry Meade–"

"I'm afraid I'm going to have to put you on hold, Mrs. Wentis, our complaints clerk, Mrs. Willis, will be with you momentarily–"

"Officer Tibbe, my husband and my son are *missing,* for God's sake–"

"I appreciate that, Mrs. Wentis, and as soon as something concrete can be done to assist you, rest assured that it will be done. You must realize, however, that since the storm began we've received at least a half dozen calls like yours, as well as numerous reports of traffic accidents–"

She hung up.

She glanced at the hall closet. Another half hour, then she'd go look for them.

She turned toward the kitchen.

And that is when she heard the small, dull thumping noises from above, from somewhere, she guessed, on the second floor.

Chapter 32

Timmy Meade remembered what his father had told him about death (two years ago, after his favorite aunt had "passed away"): "It's just a long, dreamless sleep, Timmy. No pain. Just sleep. That's what death is." It had sounded okay at the time. It had even helped a little in getting rid of the grief.

It fell flat now.

The phrase "calculated risk" came to him from somewhere in his recent past and he thought it was what he had done—he had taken a calculated risk. Because he had seen death grinning at him inside those piled-up park benches, and it had given him no choice but to head for home. Any other day, what was it?—a twenty-minute walk through woods and underbrush and, for sure, his exposed hands and sneakered feet would probably get a little frostbitten, but *that* was the calculated risk, wasn't it?

Too bad it hadn't worked.

Too bad that in the shit damn blizzard there was

no right or left, north or south, east or west. Only the snow. And the wind. And the cold.

Too bad.

He thought he was on a road. Maybe Reynolds Road. Or Sullivan's Road. (No, he decided, he couldn't have gone *that* far out of his way.) And that if he *was* on Reynolds Road it was comforting to think that it led, more or less, right back to his front door, that it was a kind of link between him and warmth. The idea made him grin a little.

And then, as if his strength had come abruptly to an end, his knees buckled, and he fell very slowly, face forward into the deep cold snow.

"Since the storm began, four hours ago"—it was the same weatherman, and he was smiling the tight, mechanical smile common to all people who are enamored of statistics—"we have registered a full twelve inches of snow. Wind gusts, as well, have been clocked at over seventy miles an hour." As if on cue, he stopped smiling. "The sheriff's department says there have been numerous traffic accidents, and a number of people have been reported missing. In some places, drifts are over ten feet high, and there are also unconfirmed reports of roofs collapsing under the strain of the wind and snow. One of the hardest-hit areas seems to be the little community of Granada, ten miles north of Penn Yann. The only road leading into Granada has been completely cut off by the storm, and residents there—and in the rest of Ontario County— are, of course, urged to stay in their homes. Although the temperature itself is staying fairly constant, at fifteen degrees Fahrenheit, the near-gale-force winds are producing wind chills in excess of forty and fifty degrees below zero, a temperature that will bring frostbite to exposed extremities within . . ."

When she had thrown the vase, and the television screen had imploded dully—showering sparks everywhere—Trudy Wentis settled herself into the nearest chair, let her head fall back, and closed her eyes lightly.

This was insanity.

This whole damned thing was sheer insanity!

This fine, new house in the middle of nowhere was insanity!

And the fact that her husband and her son were out in that damned blizzard—their noses and fingers and toes probably turning black from frostbite—was insanity!

And the idea that something was in the house with her—God knew what; she had searched everywhere and found nothing—was insanity, too!

She opened her eyes very slowly, in disbelief. The loud, frantic knocking at the front door had been going on for several minutes, she realized.

She stood. She ran to the door. Unlocked it. Threw it open.

Larry Meade and Dick Wentis stumbled through the doorway and into the house.

"Dick . . ." she managed.

He glanced blankly at her. Larry was holding him up; he was holding Larry up.

Then, as if succumbing, at last, to the weight of the snow on their backs and shoulders, and the ice crusted around their faces, they crumbled to the floor.

*   *   *

"Mr. Jenner, this is Janice McIntyre again. Is my husband still there?"

"Yes, hold on, please."

A moment's silence; "Janice? What's wrong?"

"Nothing, really. Just lonely. The storm's still pretty bad out here. I don't imagine you're planning to come home soon, are you?"

"As soon as I can, Janice. It's bad where I am, too, and from what I hear, it's not going to get any better."

"Yes, I know; I was just wondering if I should go to a neighbor's house, Miles. The Wentises live practically next door—"

"No. Please. Just stay where you are, Jan. I realize it's not far, but with the visibility as bad as it is you can become disoriented in a hurry. *I* know. I went to the car for my cigarettes—the car's just down the street—and damned if I didn't almost get lost on the way back. And if you get lost out there, Jan—"

She sighed. "Yes. Okay. I'll stay put. What does Jenner have to say about selling the house?"

"He says there should be no problem. People are really anxious to live in little rural developments like ours, apparently. 'Urban Decay,' and all that."

She smiled. "I'm glad to hear it, Miles. Thank you."

A moment's silence; then, "I'll be home when I can, Janice. I love you." And he hung up.

Chapter 33

The big Jeep Cherokee Chief—on loan from the Ontario County Sheriff to the Penn Yann police—was doing something that John Marsh believed four-wheel-drive vehicles weren't supposed to do: It was spinning its tires. It was stuck.

He hit the steering wheel with his open left hand. "Damn it!" He ruefully recalled what Matt Peters had told him:

"I appreciate your wanting to do this, John. Lord knows we've got our hands full, and if you *could* get into Granada and help out we'd surely appreciate it. But I gotta warn you, that damned Jeep's a mess—two bald tires, a cracked windshield, half the lights don't work, and the transmission's squirrely as hell. It's just about ready for the scrap heap, John, and if I didn't know you, and if I didn't think you could handle it, I'd flat out refuse. But the engine's pretty good, and the CB radio works okay, and you can always use the plow if you get into real trouble. Plus we got a report of a couple more people missing out there—Christ!—so I'll let you take it, John. Just remember, please—it's not ours."

He shoved the transmission into low reverse; he touched the accelerator gently; the truck shifted a little to the left; the tires spun madly.

"Goddamnit it all!" He hit the steering wheel again.

He turned the windshield wipers off, then the ignition.

He glanced at the three quart-sized thermos bottles filled with hot coffee, the checkered blankets piled up in back, the two well-stocked first aid kits. He really had given it his best shot, hadn't he? How was he to know this blizzard was going to be a killer?

He turned the ignition to ACC and checked the gas gauge. He cursed again. The gauge registered just over half. He'd filled the tank before leaving Penn Yann—ten damned miles on ten or twelve damned gallons of gas; the damned truck was a damned pig! But Matt Peters had warned him about that, too, hadn't he? "You know that these four-wheel-drive vehicles are not exactly what they used to call 'fuel efficient.' And this one, old as it is, and that storm being as bad as it is . . . You'll be lucky if you make it to Granada and back on a full tank, John."

Marsh remembered laughing at that.

Now he laughed again. At himself, and his stupidity.

And, when his laughter ended, he found that his eyes had focused on a squat, dark mound, barely visible through the blowing snow, on the road about ten feet in front of the truck. He realized that

someone was out there, lying face down in the
snow. He pushed the door open and scrambled
from the truck.

Norm, Marge Gellis wrote, and crossed it out.

Dear Norm,
When I was a teenager, my sister would
get me dates with boys I had never met. She
told me it was more fun to have dates with
boys you never met. She was a very pretty
girl, the type that becomes a cheerleader, which
she was, and was three years older than me. I
didn't know at the time that she was doing
me a favor by getting me these dates because
I could never have gotten them myself. Because
I was shy, and not very pretty. But me and
these blind dates did have some nice times.
And some bad times, too. But my memories of
what my sister tried to do for me then are
pretty good.
Norm, I have another blind date.

She crossed out all of it. Very firmly, and very
thoroughly. Damn it, goddamnit! Why had she
never learned to write so people could understand
her?

Dick Wentis asked his wife, "Am I all right? And
Larry?"
With great effort, Trudy had managed to get
both of them onto the big, L-shaped couch, had
stripped their wet clothes from them, and had covered them both with electric blankets set on low. It
was all she could have done, she realized now,

although they both had displayed symptoms of hypothermia—slurred speech, disorientation—and there were tiny patches of frostbite on the tips of some of their fingers and toes.

"Yes," she said to Dick. "Larry's still asleep." As she spoke, Larry's eyes fluttered open. "Dick," she continued, "you didn't find Sam?" It was a stupid question, she realized, but she had to ask it.

He sighed. "We looked ... everywhere." He took a deep breath. "It was impossible, Trudy. He could–" Another deep breath. "He could have been ten feet away, and we would have missed him." He put his hand on the back of the couch and prepared to sit up. He made it halfway, then lay down once more, breathing heavily. "I'm going out there again, Trudy. Just get some hot coffee into me ..."

"No," Trudy said with finality. Her eyes watered. She lowered her head and wept softly. "No," she murmured.

He stared incredulously at her. "Goddamnit!" He sat up quickly, and saw that Larry had already done what he—Dick—had been planning to do; because, Christ! There were other people who could help.

Larry gently set the telephone down. He was smiling. "They've found Timmy."

"Timmy?" Dick said.

"Yes. Alive. About a mile and a half down Reynolds Road. Some guy in a Jeep ..."

"What about Sam? Did they say anything about Sam?"

Larry answered, as if in apology, "No. They didn't. Just Timmy. I guess he and the guy in the Jeep are stuck where they are till the storm ends. But no, nothing about Sam. I'm sorry." He picked up the telephone again. "I've got to call Dora."

"Your line's dead, Larry." It was Trudy speaking.

He looked blankly at her a moment, then put the phone back down.

"The storm," Trudy explained. He nodded. She turned to Dick. "Nobody can help us find Sam till it's eased a little—that's what the Sheriff's Department told me."

"Uh-huh," he said resignedly; then he saw the shattered TV. He looked questioningly at his wife:

"There was someone in the house," she told him.

"Someone in the house? You mean"—he indicated the TV—"someone broke in and–"

"No. *I* did that. But there was somebody in the house."

"Maybe an animal," Dick suggested. "Getting in out of the storm?"

"I don't know. Maybe."

"Why didn't you tell me this before?"

"I checked everywhere, Dick. Every room, every closet–"

Larry Meade cut in, "Trudy, where'd you put my clothes? I've got to get home."

"In the kitchen, Larry."

He leaned over and touched Trudy's shoulder; "Thank you for everything," he said. "Sam will be okay, you'll see. He's a resourceful little kid, that's what Timmy says."

"Yes," she murmured, unconvinced; Larry went into the kitchen.

Dick took Trudy's hand. "We've got to prepare ourselves, Trudy." He felt her hand stiffen. "Because this is bad. Very bad."

She looked away and began weeping again, louder.

"It's a situation," Dick went on, "it's a set of circumstances, Trudy, that *no one* could have foreseen . . ."

Larry reappeared suddenly from the kitchen. He had his pants on—they were still damp—and was holding his shirt in his left hand. He had an urgent and quizzical look about him. "What's above your kitchen?" he asked. "Is that a bedroom?"

"Yes," Larry answered. "It's Sam's bedroom. Why?"

Larry grinned nervously. "Because there's somebody up there. I can hear them. Somebody's walking around up there."

It was bad enough not being able to hear the damned biggest storm of the century wailing away outside, Norm Gellis thought. But it was worse standing and watching it through the front window and hearing nothing. Like he'd gone deaf. He quickly drew the curtains shut.

He called to Marge again and got no answer. "Damned spook!" Hiding from the storm, probably. In a closet or something, shivering and shaking just like her little molded jellos did. Mass, for Chrissakes!

He had long since stopped hiding the .38 Police Special under the upstairs bathroom sink. He reasoned that if he really needed it, it should be easy to get to; so, for several weeks, he had kept it in the drawer of an end table beside the couch.

He thought about it now. He thought he would need it before long. And the rifles, too. Because things just didn't feel right. Like there was some vague smell in the air and you had to sniff just right to catch it, but when you did, it made you retch.

"Marge, for Chrissakes!" He yelled, expecting no answer. He got none.

Then he realized that he needed some *noise* in the house. Something to connect him with what was going on in the world. Something that would knife into the damned quiet.

He picked up the TV's remote control from the arm of his La-Z-Boy; he turned the TV on; he turned the volume up very high.

It would be good to start packing today, Janice McIntyre thought. The move to another house would seem more imminent if she saw packed boxes here and there, and if this house were half empty. Just the nonessentials, of course—there were lots of those.

She put her hand on her abdomen. No strenuous packing, though. Nothing heavy. She was convinced that was why Jodie had been born prematurely, because she'd done too much hard physical work the day before. The doctor had said she was wrong, but then the doctor had said other things too: "Jodie's the picture of health, Mrs. McIntyre," was one of the things he'd said. Damn him to hell!

She stood quietly for a minute to let her sudden anger cool. She was in the kitchen, and had made a full pot of coffee. She decided now that she didn't want any of it.

She unplugged the pot.

She left the kitchen.

She'd pack the baby's things first, she decided, and she started up the stairs.

Chapter 34

Dick Wentis threw open the door to his son's room. He raised the fireplace poker high above his head ("What do you need *that* for, Dick?" . . . "It's just a precaution, Trudy.").

But except for the bed and the dresser, a lamp, and some nondescript posters on one wall, the room was empty.

"It looks empty," Dick whispered.

Trudy shouldered herself up next to him in the doorway. "What about the bathroom, Dick?"

He looked to the left, toward the adjoining bathroom. The door was closed. "I don't know," he said.

She stuck her head into the bedroom. "I always keep that door open," she said. "Otherwise it gets stuffy in there."

Dick said nothing. He coaxed her into the hallway, stepped into the room, and turned toward the bathroom. Trudy said from the hallway, "*Sam* might be in there, Dick."

He glanced at her; she was smiling tentatively. "It's somebody, Dick. Who's to say it's not Sam?" The tentative smile flickered on and off, as if it were a nervous twitch.

"You had the front door *locked*, Trudy."

"Sam has a key, Dick." She paused, glanced at the floor; the nervous smile became stuck on her face, like a grimace. "A key," she repeated.

A moment later, she shot through the doorway, pushed past her husband, and pulled the bathroom door open. "Sam–" she yelled, as if in an ecstatic greeting.

But the bathroom was empty.

She felt Dick's hands on her shoulders. He whispered to her, "The attic, Trudy. Whoever it is is in the attic. I can hear him." He led her to Sam's bed, sat her on it, went to the door. "I'm going to go have a look," he told her.

She said, standing, "Yes, I'll come with you."

Larry Meade didn't know what he was seeing at first. He was reminded of the time, twenty years before, when a family pet had dragged itself home after being hit by a car, had managed to pull the kitchen screen door open, and had pulled itself across the floor, leaving an irregular trail of blood on the old linoleum. He had found the animal dead on the cellar stairs.

That is what he thought of now, seeing the thin, ragged trail of blood that led from the kitchen, to the hallway, and then—in little fits and starts on the thick rug—up the stairs to the second floor.

He thought, cursing himself, even as he thought it, *Jesus, Dora's had her damned period!*

He heard her voice from upstairs; "Who are you?" it said.

"Dora?" he called. "What's wrong?"

"Who are you?" the voice repeated. "What do you want?"

He noticed for the first time that it was getting dark in the house. He reached for the light switch at the bottom of the stairs and called again, as he flicked it on, "Dora?"

The house stayed dark.

"Damn it!" he whispered. "Are you okay, Dora?" he called. "Dora, they've found Timmy. Some guy in a Jeep out on Reynolds Road found him." He waited. He heard giggling.

He leaned over and fingered some of the blood on the stairs; it was just starting to coagulate. He straightened. "Dora, is somebody up there with you?"

"What do you want?" he heard again.

He started up the stairs. "Dora?"

And that is when they appeared. At the top of the stairs. Instantly. As if they had been there all along and the rapid change in the light had finally revealed them. Two boys. Three girls. Naked, blank-faced, blue-eyed, dark-haired. And each so exquisitely, so perfectly, and so impossibly beautiful that Larry gasped upon seeing them:

He stumbled backward, groping for the knob on the front door. He found it and threw the door open.

Dearest Norm. Marge Gellis crossed it out furiously.

Dear Norm. She crossed that out, too.

She realized suddenly that she hadn't yet decided

exactly how she was going to do it, what she had to do, and that was very important, because she wanted no pain. Only a slow and peaceful separation. Something pleasant.

> *Norm,*
>   *You won't understand. I won't even ask you to understand.*

She crossed it out. She reached to her right to turn on the deskside lamp. The lamp wouldn't work. Mechanically, out of habit, she jiggled it a little. The bulb flickered briefly, then lit.

When he was a young man, Dick Wentis put in several years as an insulation contractor. It hadn't worked out because his business sense was on a much lower level than his ambition, but the work had helped him to overcome a weak feeling of claustrophobia, because he had to make his way through attics which, in new homes, sometimes allowed no more than two or three feet of clearance between ceiling and floor.

He thought of those years now as he positioned a stepladder under the attic access panel in the closet of the master bedroom. He said to Trudy, as he climbed the stepladder, "It has to be an animal. Maybe it got in through the roof vents, I don't know." He seemed irritated. He put his hands on the panel; he pushed hard. "Damn it!" he breathed.

"What's the matter?" Trudy asked; she was holding the stepladder.

"It's stuck," he answered. He took his hands from the panel. "This is fucking stupid!" he said.

"No," Trudy said. "It isn't."

He glanced questioningly at her.

"Sam's gone up there before," she told him quietly. "A couple times. I don't know, I guess it's like a fort or something—" She stopped; she was making foolish excuses for him, she realized. Excuses Dick could not possibly accept.

"You never told me," he said.

"I didn't know what your reaction would be, Dick."

He exhaled; "We'll talk about it later." Then, abruptly, he put his hands on the panel once more. He pushed. The panel gave easily. He slid it to one side. Bits of gray, cellulose insulation drifted onto his hair and shoulders. Some got into his right eye and he rubbed the eye angrily.

He took another step up the ladder and stuck his head into the dark attic. He waited a moment; then, "I'll need a light, Trudy."

"Can you see anything?"

"No, that's why I need the light."

"Dick, this is stupid, like you said. How *could* he have gotten up there without me knowing? And besides, that stuff, that insulation, would be all over the closet. Maybe we should both go looking for him outside again, Dick—"

He turned his head sharply to look at her, his facial muscles tight. "I can hear him, Trudy, I can hear him breathing."

"My God!"

"Please get me the light. *Now!*"

She went hurriedly into the bedroom, unplugged one of the bedside lamps. "Dick," she called, "this cord's not going to be long enough."

He called back, "There are a couple of extension

cords in the kitchen. Get me the longest one you can find."

"Yes," she said, and she set the lamp down and left the room.

Dick stuck his head into the attic again. He listened.

The breathing (if that's what it was, he thought; because it could just as easily have been the roof moving slightly in the wind, or snow being pushed into the vents) seemed to come from several different directions, depending on which way he moved his head. And it seemed very shallow and rapid, as if whoever was up there was not only out of breath, but was trying hard to hide himself, too.

"Sam?" He kept his voice low and soothing. "It's me. Your father. Are you up here, Sam?" He listened. The breathing seemed to alter pitch slightly. He smiled. "Sam, please come down out of there. We're worried sick about you."

The breathing stopped.

"Sam?" He heard low scuffling noises far to his right, near the attic's east wall. "Sam? Is that you? Please, Sam, don't be afraid." He listened.

He heard the breathing again, but to his left. And it was very close.

He turned his head. He squinted into the darkness. He said very tentatively—because he wasn't sure what he was seeing, or if he was seeing anything at all—"Sam? Is that you?"

Trudy, taking him by surprise, said from behind him, "Here's the lamp, Dick."

He felt heat near his thigh; he turned his head. Trudy was handing the lamp to him, minus its shade. "The extension cord should be long enough, Dick. Be careful up there. Please."

He reached for the lamp. "Trudy, he's here. Sam's here. I know it." He looked quizzically at her. "What's wrong, Trudy?" Her mouth had dropped open slightly; her eyes had widened. "Trudy?" He saw that she was looking at something behind him, in the access hole.

He looked. "Holy Mother of Jesus!" he hissed, and felt himself falling backward from the stepladder. He threw his arms wide.

Trudy screamed.

And Sam Wentis, naked, a look of stark and awful confusion about him, his face and body riddled with small, ugly, dark brown splotches—like a dying plant—leaped from the access hole to the floor of the closet:

Dick, still falling, tried to cushion himself with his arms and hands, but the closet was too cramped, and his fall too uncontrolled. He hit the floor first with his back, his left arm slipped beneath him, twisted, broke at the elbow; then his forehead slammed into the doorframe. He made a small, dry hacking noise—all he could manage through the enormous, sudden pain—then passed into unconsciousness.

And, while Trudy continued to scream shrilly, in agony for the thing which had once been her adoptive son, Sam Wentis fled the room and was gone.

Chapter 35

Larry Meade turned the car radio on, listened for a moment to a Paul Simon oldie, turned it off. It was good, he thought suddenly, that Timmy had gotten out of Granada. There was no real need for him to stay.

The car's four doors were locked; he had thrown the garage door open for ventilation, and so the garage was dusted everywhere with snow, though lightly, because the winds were from the north, and the garage faced east. He could see nothing through the thin layer of snow on the car's windows.

A half hour earlier, when he had stumbled into the garage, he had figured out that if he ran the engine just ten or fifteen minutes an hour, for the heat, then he had a good five or six hours left.

But everything had changed, since then. Slowly, but immutably, everything had changed.

Because his understanding had changed. Profoundly.

Because, when he had seen the children at the

tree line, he had caught a fleeting and inner glimpse of what they were, and of what they were capable of. And that glimpse—brief as it had been—had frightened him more than he had ever been frightened, the cold, nervous fear that is caused by ignorance. A fear which had, in the last hour, given way to knowledge.

He wanted desperately to tell someone what he knew, what he understood, so they would understand, too. Dick Wentis, maybe. Or Trudy. Someone. "I've seen them, and I know what they are!" But he couldn't really say what they were, he realized. Only that they were of the earth. That they had a purpose. And that they needed him.

He put his head down so his forehead rested against the top of the steering wheel. He whispered, "I'm sorry." He didn't know precisely to whom he was whispering it—to his wife, perhaps, whom he'd abandoned. Or maybe to himself—to the civilized man cringing deep inside him in stark fear of what he was going to do in the next few seconds.

He put his hand on the door handle. He gripped it hard. The civilized man inside him screamed, *What are you doing?! What are you doing?! You've got to fight them!* And, smiling benignly, he answered himself, *I've fought them all my life. I'm done fighting them.*

And with one quick, smooth motion he opened the door and stepped out of the car.

His peripheral vision showed him that the children were waiting. He turned his head; he looked at them; he saw the great hunger, and the overwhelming need in their eyes.

And he realized at once, and almost joyfully, that they were stronger, and better, than him.

He inhaled very deeply; he felt the cold air moving into his lungs; he imagined that he could feel his lungs swelling in response.

It was the last work his lungs ever did. The children were on him in a second, and they brought death to him as quickly and as mercifully as they had to Dora.

And afterward, before eating, they touched his body with their own special kind of trembling and silent gratitude for the offering he had made of himself.

Chapter 36

Night

"The TV says the storm should end pretty soon, Miles. Maybe you could come home then."

She heard him sigh. "There's another storm right on top of this one, Jan. We'll get a breather of maybe an hour or two, then it'll start all over again. I'm going to have to stay put at least until morning. Just make sure everything's closed up tight—"

"I've got all the windows and doors locked, Miles. And I've been packing the baby's things, too. We had some boxes left over from when we moved in—"

"Aren't you jumping the gun a little?"

"Uh-huh. A little. It's good therapy, though."

"Therapy?"

"Keeps my mind off . . . other things—" She didn't want to elaborate for fear of a lecture. She got one, anyway.

"Janice, this storm, and you being alone there, is

perfect for this . . . delusion you're preoccupied with. Why don't you just read, or listen to some music, or watch TV–"

"I could talk to you for the rest of the night, Miles."

"I wish you could, but I can't tie up Jenner's phone." He paused. She heard Jenner say something to him. He came on the line again. "Jan, he wants to call his parents. They live on some little out-of-the-way farm, apparently, and were supposed to call him every hour on the hour. They missed their last call, so I'll have to say goodbye for now. I'll call you again when I get the chance. I love you."

Janice began, "I love . . ." But he had already hung up.

She scowled a little. He was right, of course. For her own peace of mind she had better occupy herself with *something*.

She went into the kitchen, opened a drawer, fished around in the confusion of electrical parts, solder, old kitchen knives, thread, and other essentially useless things, until she found a small screwdriver.

She'd take the crib apart now. That's what she'd do.

Norm Gellis had heard the soft tapping at the front windows, the scratching noises at the doors. He thought that Joe had wandered back and wanted to get in, so he'd checked, but had found nothing. And now, in his La-Z-Boy, with the .38 in his lap, and the TV on, but the volume off, he could *feel* that he and Marge were not the only living things in the house. He liked that feeling. He grinned hugely. Confrontation, at last—it was just around the corner.

He heard a dull thump from above—from the guest bedroom. His grin, huge as it was, broadened even more. Let the little bastards come to him!

He was ready for them.

Pills, of course, Marge decided. Because they would carry her off gently. Because they could soothe her into death, could cradle her into it.

In the downstairs bathroom there were pills. Lots of them. There were sleeping pills, and diet pills (which Norm used on occasion), and pain pills (if you had the right kind of pain) . . .

Dear Norm,
I am going to take some pills.

She crossed it out, wadded the paper up, put it into the pocket of her housedress.

She listened. She wished Norm would stop moving around outside her closed door. She wished he would go back downstairs. She didn't want to see him, not even one last time.

When Janice first noticed the faint odor of woodsmoke, and the noxious smell of burning hair, she tried to tell herself that she was smelling nothing more, perhaps, than the odor of her perfume mixed with her own sweat.

She was in the upstairs hallway, on her way to the baby's room (what would have *been* the baby's room, she corrected herself); the two overhead lights were on; the hallway was brightly lighted, and she clutched the small screwdriver very tightly in her hand.

She heard a woman's voice. Though faintly, as if water were clogging her ears, and the woman was whispering, "No, Janice, not here, not tonight."

She stopped walking. She heard the screwdriver clatter to the floor. She said "Rachel?" tremblingly.

The smell of woodsmoke and burning hair grew stronger, until it turned her stomach and brought bile into her mouth.

"Rachel?" she said again. She waited. She heard nothing.

The sudden grip on her shoulder was very light, as if she had walked under someone's outstretched hand. "Rachel?" she said again, and she saw that the baby's room was directly to her left, that, in the light from the hallway, she could see the crib against the north wall.

And something was in the crib, she saw—something was crouching in it.

She gasped.

The touch at her shoulder strengthened. The odors of woodsmoke and burning hair moved around her like a fluid and made her eyes sting.

Then, through it all, she saw the thing in the crib straighten, and stand. "I could talk to you for the rest of the night, Miles," it said.

And at the same time, the strong hand on her shoulder pushed her violently from the room, down the hall, to the top of the stairs. "No," Janice murmured. "No, Rachel, please . . ."

It was a cold grip, and firm, and the awful smells that accompanied it were like a physical presence.

It held her at the top of the stairs; and the

woman's voice whispered urgently, "Run, Janice! Run from here!"

She heard the flames, then. From behind her. From the baby's room.

She turned her head. She saw the flames. They danced hotly and quickly around the door to the baby's room.

Then they leaped forward into the hallway.

Janice screamed. And heard again, through the scream, "Run, Janice! Run from here!" The grip on her shoulder stopped; she felt a soft, cold hand on her back coax her firmly down the stairs.

She stopped screaming. Very stiffly, in disbelief, and in awe, she descended the stairs, one hand on the wall for support, because the smoke from the fire in the hallway above was curling around her, cutting off her vision, and her air, and she was beginning to feel faint.

She began to cough. Softly at first, as if in a denial of what was happening, then loudly, from deep within her chest, because the smoke had thickened and blackened. Then, at last—though futilely—the smoke and fire alarms sounded, their bright, mechanical squeals barely audible beneath the loud rushing noises of the flames.

She found herself in front of the hall closet. She pulled the door open, reached in, yanked out one of her winter coats, wrestled it from the hanger, threw the coat around herself.

She looked to her right. Up the stairs.

And saw through the smoke, against the bright backdrop of the flames, that Rachel Griffin—tall, dark-haired, pretty—was smiling at her. As if pleased.

Janice's mouth opened. She could say nothing. She thought, with deep affection, *Thank you*.

And in sudden panic, she fled the house.

The night was very clear, and very still, and very cold.

She ran to her right, through varying depths of drifted snow, over lawns, and driveways, and backyards, toward Granada's gate.

Chapter 37

Norm Gellis had a mental image of himself surrounded by his guns. He liked the image. It made him feel somehow like a whole man, and worth something. Not just to himself, but to Marge as well, and to all the others who couldn't admit that a danger really did exist.

The Weatherby 20 gauge—retrieved long before from the spot where Malcolm Harris had dropped it—was leaning barrel up against the right arm of the chair. The Remington 760 leaned against the chair's left arm. He held the pistol in his lap. All the weapons were loaded.

Marge had appeared a half hour earlier, headed—for reasons she had not shared—to the large downstairs bathroom. On her way back, something clutched in her left hand, he had told her, "Ever heard of a siege, Marge? Well, this is a siege. And I'm ready for it."

"Yes," she whispered, and went back upstairs.

"Damned spook!" he said now. Shit, it was way

past time to cut her loose, wasn't it? To let her drift. It was at moments like this, he thought—when a man's life peaked, really, because he had to concentrate hard on what threatened it—that he found out who was with him, and who wasn't.

And of course he realized he was all alone. Except for the others. Those who talked and giggled and screeched, but at a distance. As they were doing at that moment. As they had been doing for a long while.

He listened. He tried again to understand individual words and sentences. But he couldn't. There were so many voices, so many pitches, and so many inflections. As if all the inhabitants of Granada had pushed into the house, into its walls and floors, and under the furniture, and they were all trying to tell him something.

He was alone except for them.

And he knew they were biding their time. Waiting for his resolve to slip. For sleep to overcome him. Then they would come out of the walls and floors and from under the furniture. And they would take him.

"Do it!" he hissed suddenly. "Bastards! Do it! Show your damned selves!"

And one did:

Sam Wentis—the creature which had once been Sam Wentis—reached out and touched him very gently and wonderingly.

Norm Gellis raised the .38. He aimed it. He fired.

The bullet passed cleanly through the creature's heart.

Reflexively, the creature ran to the front door,

pulled it open. And collapsed there, the life gone from it.

The others in the house quieted at once.

Norm Gellis stared silently at the crumpled, naked form in the doorway. He wanted to know what he had done. What he had killed. And why. He put the .38 on the floor beside the chair. "Marge?" he called. "I got him. Through the heart. Beautiful!"

He stood. Quietly and quickly he crossed the room to where the body lay. He put the toe of his shoe into the creature's belly and rolled the creature over:

The creature's mouth fell open. Some blood bubbled out of it.

"Jesus God!" Norm murmured.

And then he heard, "You son of a bitch! You've killed him, you've fucking killed him!" And he felt himself being pushed heavily away from the body to the floor.

He looked up. Dick Wentis, one arm in a sling, his head bandaged, stood quivering over him, his one good hand clenched into a tight fist, spittle around the edges of his mouth.

"No," Norm started. "I didn't . . . I mean . . ." And he felt Dick's foot connect hard with his back. He screamed in pain and pushed himself backward, in a twisted kind of crabwalk, toward the La-Z-Boy. Dick followed stiffly, and silently, his anger too intense for speech.

Norm, groping blindly with his left hand, found the butt of the .38 far sooner than he'd hoped:

He hesitated. This man above him had a right to be angry, he told himself. This man had a right to kick him into the middle of next week!

"Dick," Norm breathed, "Jesus, I'm sorry, Dick."

And in the span of that breath, he flipped the .38 around. And fired it.

Very quickly, Dick Wentis crumpled to the floor. Dead.

And, at the front door, over the body of her adopted son, Trudy Wentis screamed.

"No," Norm Gellis whispered. "It's–" And he fired the gun once more. Trudy's hand quivered at her throat. She looked very surprised. Then the surprise left her; she let her hand drop; she lowered herself slowly, and placed her body protectively over Sam's body.

His name gurgled from her mouth. And she died.

"You shoulda seen it, Marge. You shoulda been there. I was quick, Marge. Split-second quick." He paused; Marge lay very quietly. The pills had long since done their work. "Blam! Blam! Blam! It was Dick Wentis, Marge. And his wife. And their kid— what's his name? Their kid, Sam. He had a disease or something. He must've. He was all covered with sores. A social disease, I'll bet, the way kids carry on." He paused again; he heard that the others in the house had come back. And they were louder, closer. He glanced toward the door. He saw two of them there. A boy and a girl. Waiting. Another—a boy—stood near the closet. "Time," Norm said. "Just a few minutes." They said nothing. He turned back to his wife. "It always happens that way, don't it, Marge? The ones you never suspect, the ones you think are your friends–"

He saw the note Marge had left for him on the bedside table. He picked it up.

Dearest Norm, it read. *I need* And that was all.

He let it flutter to the rug.

He lowered his head. He thought he was going to cry.

He felt a small warm hand on the back of his neck, another at his stomach, another at his chest. "Yeah," he murmured. "Okay, if you gotta."

And they took him very quickly. And very gently.

From *The Rochester Democrat and Chronicle*, December 15:

BIZARRE TRAGEDY IN SOUTHERN TIER
BAFFLES INVESTIGATORS

The death toll now stands at 16 in what appears to be a baffling series of mutilation murders, suicides, and arsons in the newly developed community of Granada, ten miles north of Penn Yann. At least half of the deaths involve children, investigators say, many of whom may have succumbed to the great blizzard which passed through the area several days ago.

According to Chief of Police John Hastings, some of the children involved were either "runaways" or "perhaps relatives of people living in Granada," because, Hastings says, "our records indicate that only three or four children, at most, were full-time residents of Granada, and one of them has already been accounted for." That child, Hastings told this reporter, is 10-year-old Timmy Meade, whose parents, Dora and Larry Meade, aged 30 and 32 respectively, were among the victims in Granada.

Only two other residents of Granada appear to have escaped the incredible violence there. Miles McIntyre, 35, and his wife Janice, 29, who is, with Timmy Meade, listed in satisfactory condition at Myers Community Hospital, suffering from exposure. John Marsh, a resident of Penn Yann, found both Mrs. McIntyre, and the Meade boy, on Reynolds Road, the night of the tragedy. Marsh himself was treated for exposure at Myers Community Hospital and released. He was not available for comment.

Investigators theorize that the tragedy may have begun with the murders of Dick Wentis, 37, and his wife Trudy, 32, who were found . . .

Chapter 38

April 23, the next year

Seth Freeman liked being back where his roots were. Despite the memories. And the impulses. But he could control them now. He could turn them on, he could turn them off, and the man he called Grandpa had no reason to run from him, as he had run five years ago, when he feared that Seth—glimpsing his origins, glimpsing the *thing* that he was—was going to turn on him.

And, Seth thought now, he might have turned on him, almost did, in fact. But at last, what he had glimpsed of himself had frightened him, and quieted him. Totally. Until a week ago. When, finally, he had accepted himself for what he was— the magnificent, exquisite, and magical thing that he was.

He turned to the man beside him. "You think the people will ever try to come back here, Grandpa?" And he nodded meaningfully at the big iron gates.

The man raised an eyebrow. "Would you like it if they came back?" he asked.

Seth thought about the question for a long while. Finally, he answered, "No. This is only where it began. It is no place."

And the man understood.

From *The Rochester Times Union,* June 24—two years later:

MISSING WOMAN MAY HAVE HAD
UNDERWORLD CONNECTIONS

Liliane Muir, 29, missing since June 1, may have been the victim of an underworld-style execution, according to Rochester Chief of Detectives Bill Hammer. Ms. Muir, an employee of Dutton Labs in Rochester, was apparently planning to come forward with testimony in the death late last November of Sammy "The Pistol" Guillermo. According to Detective Hammer, Ms. Muir contacted him early in May about "certain evidence and eyewitness testimony relating to the Guillermo murder" which, Hammer went on, "will obviously have to wait quite some time—until we have an idea what happened to Ms. Muir—before it sees the light of day."

Ms. Muir, described as "short, blonde, and, when last seen, wearing blue jeans and a purple, bulky knit sweater," disappeared while visiting her sister, Ann, who lives near Eagle Bay, in the Adirondacks, about forty miles northeast of Utica, N.Y. Ms. Muir's sister testified that Ms. Muir "just went out for a walk that evening and never came back." A week-long search for the woman turned up nothing, and Detective Hammer admits now that while the chances are "very good" that she was the victim of a gangland-style killing, there seems also to have been an increase in disappearances in that area of the Adirondacks in recent months, leading to the possibility that underworld activities may have little, if any, connection with the disappearance of Ms. Muir.

From *The Inlet Bee*—one year later:

LEPRECHAUNS IN THE ADIRONDACKS?
It's the silly season again, folks. We've got monsters in Loch Ness, Big Foot in Montana, UFOs over Utah, ghosts just about everywhere, and now, as sure as the day is long, Leprechauns in the Adirondacks. That's right— Leprechauns. The Little People!

leprechaun: Irish Folklore—a fairy in the form of a little old man who can reveal a buried crock of gold to anyone who catches him.

That's the dictionary definition, folks. We, however, seem to have our own brand of leprechaun—wonderfully unique to the Adirondacks. First of all, he's not old. He is, in fact, quite young. And no one's said anything about "crocks of gold" either (although we're waiting, and hoping). Oh, and just to keep the record straight, our Adirondack Leprechauns seem to have left their clothes somewhere—

they're all quite naked. I give you this in all
sincerity, and although I am honor bound not
to name names, I can tell you that a certain
mayor of a certain little Adirondack town we
all know and love has reported seeing these
quick-moving little heathens, and also the
owner/manager of a certain favorite hardware
store . . .

But I go too far. I would, in signing off,
merely like to note that our particular Leprechaun File is circular, and that it sits on the
floor close to my desk.

Have a Happy!